Out From This Place

Other Avon Camelot Books by
Joyce Hansen

WHICH WAY FREEDOM?

JOYCE HANSEN teaches special education and enjoys photography when she isn't writing for young people. Winner of the Spirit of Detroit Award, the author's other titles include *The Gift Giver, Home Boy,* and *Which Way Freedom?* Ms. Hansen lives with her husband in New York City.

Out From This Place

JOYCE HANSEN

AN AVON  CAMELOT BOOK

AVON BOOKS, INC.
1350 Avenue of the Americas
New York, New York 10019

Copyright © 1988 by Joyce Hansen
Published by arrangement with Walker and Company
Library of Congress Catalog Card Number: 88-5594
ISBN: 0-380-71409-4
RL: 5.1
www.avonbooks.com

First Avon Camelot Printing: February 1992

CAMELOT TRADEMARK REG. U.S. PAT. OFF. AND IN OTHER COUNTRIES, MARCA REGISTRADA, HECHO EN U.S.A.

Printed in the U.S.A.

OPM 10 9 8 7

Author's Note

The people and events in *Out From This Place* are fictional but are based on incidents that occurred during the end of the Civil War, the turbulent period that witnessed the beginnings of a new people, not quite African after the two-hundred-year sojourn in the New World, not yet Americans. Only after the passage of the Thirteenth and Fourteenth amendments to the Constitution were people of African descent accorded citizenship under the law.

In 1861, when the Union army gained control of the Sea Islands off the coast of South Carolina, most of the planters fled to the mainland. Blacks became contraband, passing along with other confiscated Confederate property into the hands of the army. They continued to labor on the abandoned plantations working, for wages, for the federal government.

In January of 1865, General William T. Sherman ordered that the newly freed men and women should be settled on tracts of land on the islands off the Carolina coast extending to the "country bordering the St. Johns River, Florida." Forty thousand people were relocated in this region and were given temporary title to the abandoned lands formerly held by the Confederates. No more than forty acres of land were to be given to a family.

In May of the same year, President Andrew Johnson changed this policy, and the land was returned to the former owners. Some blacks, refusing to give back their acreage, armed themselves and fought to keep the land until they were forcibly removed by the army.

There were cases, especially in South Carolina, where

freedmen were able to purchase land, when someone was willing to sell to them or when the South Carolina Land Commission made plots available for sale, and form their own communities. New Canaan, in *Out From This Place*, is based on an all-black community in South Carolina, developed after the Civil War.

Prologue

May 1862

The young girl and the old woman sat side by side on a rug made from grass and palmetto fronds. The girl's homespun trousers stopped just above her ankles and bare feet; her thick hair was cut short. The woman's small, black, bony face was framed by a clean white cloth tightly wrapped around her head. The woman's husband sat on a scratched bench near the door of the tiny cabin.

The woman and the girl, who was about fourteen years old, wrapped palmetto fronds around blades of grass, making rugs like the one they sat on. A peal of laughter from the soldiers outside broke the silence inside the cabin. The woman stopped working and stared at the girl. "Easter, stay in the camp with us. You close to freedom here."

Easter continued making a circular pattern out of the frond and blades of grass. She and the woman had had this conversation many times before, but Easter's mind was made up. She was leaving. "I have to go back and find Jason, Mariah," she said. "My eyes see him all the time and my ears hear him. How he cry when me and Obi leave. How I promise I come back for him."

Her only memories were of her life of enslavement on the Jennings farm, near Charleston, South Carolina. Her only family, although they were not relatives, were Obi and Jason, also slaves on the farm. Easter didn't know her exact age or where she came from or who her parents were. When a young child, she had been given as an Easter present to Martha Jennings.

Obi and Easter's careful plans to run away to the Sea Islands off the Carolina coast had been thwarted, and they'd had to leave the farm without Jason. Easter, disguised as a boy, had headed to the coast with Obi. They had been captured by Confederate soldiers and forced to work in the army camp.

Mariah picked up her work again. "Ask the Colonel to let you stay here. One of the field hands tell me there'll be only fifty soldiers left in this camp when the regiment leave. You could be the servant boy for the new colonel." She winked at Easter. "I know the Colonel say yes. What he care about one slave boy when he have Yankee to fight?"

"Woman, think you know everything?" the man muttered as he cleaned his ax.

"I know how white peoples think, Gabriel. That's why I still livin'."

Easter's bright brown eyes nearly closed when she smiled. She rubbed her forehead. "Don't y'all be fussin'. I leavin' with the Colonel. I the one who beg him to take me to Charleston. I tell him I only want to work for him. When we near Charleston I runnin' from the camp and I find the Jennings farm."

"Suppose you don't find it," Mariah said as she pulled hard on the palmetto frond.

"I find it. I go to the Phillips plantation, where Master Jennings hire me and Obi out to work. All I have to do is ask someone where the Phillips plantation is. Everyone know it."

Mariah sucked her teeth loudly. "Suppose you ask the wrong someone. You know them patterollers still beatin' and arrestin' runaways. You foolish. The work here be easy when the regiment leave. All we have to do is duck when they start firin' them cannon at the Yankee boats."

"Got to get Jason," Easter repeated softly. "He waitin'."

"It's a year since you leave."

"I know. He waitin' still," she said.

"Guess I save my breath to pray with. Your mind is set," Mariah mumbled. She picked up more grass, intertwining one blade with another.

Easter's smooth chestnut brown face looked older than her years. "Jason mother die when he born," she said, "and Mistress Jennings make me take care of him from that time on."

"If you stay here, you could escape 'cross the river like Obi did and get on the island with the Yankee," Mariah insisted.

"Thought you was savin' your breath to pray with," Gabriel muttered.

Easter's mind drifted back to the day Obi escaped. Mariah interrupted her thoughts. "He 'cross that river thinkin' about you right now," she said.

Gabriel rubbed his wiry gray beard. "Lord, woman, you even know what peoples 'cross the river thinkin'?"

"Why don't you and Gabriel go to the island, Mariah?" Easter asked, trying to change the subject.

"When Master send me here to work for these Confederates, it the happiest day of my sad life." Mariah laughed bitterly. "I free long as I don't have no mistress in my face day and night screechin' after me. I don't want to see another rice plantation long as I live. Them Yankee have to get on this side of the river if they want to free me." Her high cheekbones seemed to jut defiantly out of her face.

"After I find Jason, I get to Obi. And you and Gabriel comin' with us." Easter's mind drifted again to the day Obi left the camp, the way he held her and kissed her, the way his long slender waist felt enclosed in her arms. He'd always been like an older brother; she had no words for her new feelings about Obi. But first she had to find Jason.

Gabriel narrowed his tired-looking red eyes. "Suppose the family ain't there no more?" he asked. "Didn't you say they movin' to the West?"

"They wasn't takin' Jason. Mistress tell me they was givin' him as a wedding present to Missy Holmes, or maybe they sell him."

"How you find him if he sold?" Gabriel asked.

"Maybe they sell him to one of the farmers nearby," Easter replied.

"Maybe they sell him to someone clear 'cross the country," Mariah snapped.

Easter refused to be discouraged. "Then I go clear 'cross the country to find him," she said.

Mariah's small slanted eyes moistened as she peered closely at Easter. "You like a tough little nail, gal. I still see the day them soldier drag you and Obi into this camp. We goin' to miss you."

Easter dropped her work and embraced Mariah. Mariah cupped Easter's dainty, heart-shaped face in her hands. "Be careful, gal. Pray. Most time only God be listenin'."

Easter gazed at the gray mists rising from the river and at the small figure of Mariah; her cloth enveloped her head like a swirl of white clouds. Mariah waved, and Easter kept looking back until she could no longer see her. Mariah, the huts, and the cannons lining the riverfront seemed to all be washed away by the gray mists, which were becoming a heavy downpour.

The procession of soldiers, horses, caissons, supply wagons, and black laborers crawled down the road. Easter clutched the grass rug that Mariah had given her, a design of squares decorated with pine needles. Besides the army shirt, the trousers, and the straw hat she wore, the rug was her only possession. She was a small figure trudging alongside the wagon that held the Colonel's cooking utensils, food, and other supplies. She kept her distance as best she could from the foulmouthed soldiers and the other blacks, who were all male. They took care of the supply wagons and the animals and would build the fortifications and dig the rifle pits when the regiment settled into a new camp.

The blacks called her Ezra or "the Colonel's boy" to her face. She knew that behind her back they called her "the Colonel's sissy." She hoped that no one found out that she wasn't a girlish boy but a real girl.

Her fears eased as they sloshed along the wet roads. Everyone concentrated on keeping dry and mud-free. That night Easter spread Mariah's rug on the ground. The Colonel gave her a piece of oilcloth to cover herself with, but her clothing remained wet. The rags she'd tied around her feet for the journey were filthy and soaked. She curled herself practically into a ball, but nothing she did made her comfortable. Rocks, small stones, and branches jabbed her no matter how she lay. Only by staring at the bright stars, thinking about Jason, and reliving Obi's embrace did she manage to fall into a fitful sleep.

The days were a blur of soldiers in wide, dirty slouch hats and forage caps with the stars and bars on them, laborers in overalls and straw hats, muskets, shotguns, haversacks, boots, steel-toed brogans, tents, mules, horses, caissons, and gun carriages, their metal clanking and scraping over the ground. Her senses were assaulted by the pungent smell of men and animals. Mud. Heat. Flies and mosquitoes. Her own body sore and stiff and beginning to smell sour also.

Finally one night she overheard a soldier say, "We just outside of Charleston." It was her time to leave. She gazed at the camp and couldn't imagine herself going alone into the darkness that spread beyond the campfires. With only memories of being a slave, she had no idea until now how a helpless child must feel.

Nervous, she was beginning to prepare the Colonel's evening coffee when she heard shouting as several soldiers and laborers came roaring into the camp. "We havin' a feast tonight," one of the soldiers yelled. Two black men carried a pig hanging upside down with its legs tied around a stick. The whole camp burst into cheers.

"You been stealin' from these farmers 'round here?" a sergeant asked roughly, but with a wide grin on his face.

"No sir, we ain't been stealin'," a soldier answered. "We was *foragin'* for wild berries and possum, sir, when this here pig come in our path. We thought it was a Yankee, sir, so we shoot it."

The camp exploded into laughter. By the time Easter served the Colonel his coffee, cleaned the coffee boiler, and finished a few other chores, the smell of roasting pig filled her nostrils. The smoke and the smell reminded her of the Jennings farm. *I bet the farm near here,* she said to herself. She watched the men stoking the fire and giving instructions to the black cook, who ignored them. She listened to the laughing and the rude jokes and tried to find the strength to leave. There were farms nearby, and the camp was near Charleston. There was every chance that she was close to the Jennings farm.

Easter stared at the sparkling night sky. She'd always liked to watch the stars. She used to tell Jason that stars were really the angels smiling down on the world. The thought made her less afraid. *Is God up there?* she wondered. Was God peeping down at her, listening to her, like Mariah said?

She had the stars and she had God. Easter rolled up her rug and walked away from the Colonel's tent, past the shouting, cursing, rollicking men. She walked past the circle of campfires. She didn't even run—simply walked away, and no one noticed. But once darkness covered her, she raced through the night with a heart and mind empty of every feeling and thought except fear. The noise from the camp gradually faded into the sounds of the forest. She ran, trying to break through her wall of panic with prayer. Each time the panic threatened to paralyze her, she prayed and glanced at the stars, imagining God.

She ran until she heard the sound of a barking hound, knowing that meant the possibility of a nearby farm. Easter stumbled toward the sound on numb feet, until she could run no longer. Spreading her rug on the ground, she lay down and fell into a troubled sleep.

She didn't wake up until she felt sharp jabs to her shoulders and thighs. Opening her eyes, she stared into a dirty, blond beard.

CHAPTER
ONE

Yes, Ethiopia yet shall stretch
Her bleeding hands abroad;
Her cry of agony shall reach
Up to the throne of God.

Frances E. W. Harper

"You a runaway?" the man asked. "What you doin' here?"

"Nothing, suh," Easter said, scrambling up quickly off the ground. The man's battered hat shaded his eyes. He pointed a shotgun in her face. His hound sat quietly at his feet. "I lost," she added as she bent down and picked up her hat, keeping one eye on the shotgun.

"Lost? How you get lost? Is you a boy or girl?"

"A boy. Name Ezra," she answered, avoiding his eyes. "My master send me to work for the soldiers. Me and some of the other boys was foraging for food for the camp. They go one way and I go another. I come from 'round here, and I want to visit my master." She thought about Jason, and tears welled up convincingly in her eyes. "I love my master and I want to see him." Her full mouth trembled slightly.

"Who your master?"

"John Jennings, suh. He have a tobacco farm near here."

"Never hear of no John Jennings."

Her heart sank. "You know Master Phillips? He have a big plantation, and my master sell tobacco to him."

"There's a good-size plantation about five miles from here, I think."

Finding the Phillips plantation would be as good as getting to the farm. She knew many of the people there and could get information about Jason. The man kept his gun trained on her. "You sure you ain't no runaway? I could use some help 'round my farm." He moved closer to her, and the dog stood up. She backed away from him.

"No, suh. I ain't no runaway. Tryin' to get to my master is all. Where you say the plantation is? If I find the plantation, I find my master farm easy."

He ignored her question. "You look hungry. I'll give you some food, then you help me. Then I'll let you go."

"Oh no, suh. Have to go now." She knew that if she ran, he'd probably fire his gun at her and the dog would give chase. Worry lines creased her forehead. "Please, suh. I have to see my master now. Then I go back to the soldiers. I belong to the Confederates. Otherwise I be glad to help you."

He hesitated and stopped moving toward her.

"Suh, I the property of the Confederates," she repeated, since that seemed to make him somewhat nervous. "Just want to see my master 'fore the soldiers come look for me. The soldiers near here, so could you tell me where the big plantation is?" she pleaded.

"Get out of here and head yonder." He pointed toward a field edged with tall pines. "I don't want trouble with them soldiers."

Easter sped off before the farmer changed his mind. She didn't care about the danger of running in the daytime. She raced across the field toward the pines and found herself back in the woods. Hoping she wasn't going around in a circle, she followed the odor of burning wood, which led her out of the forest and brought her face to face with a large expanse of cotton fields. Male and female hands were hoeing the dirt around the rows of plants. There seemed to be too few workers for the fields that had to be hoed. Easter rubbed her throbbing head. Although most cotton fields looked alike, there was something familiar about this one.

She knew that across the fields there were peach orchards, and there were live oak trees lining the avenue to the large two-story house where the Phillips family lived. She also knew that behind the big house a footpath led to the slave cabins. This had to be the Phillips plantation.

Easter plopped down onto the ground and cried and laughed all at once. The road that led to the Jennings farm was on the other side of the big house. Before going to the farm, though, she'd look for her friend Rose, who was the cook's helper. Rose would be able to give her all of the news and could probably tell her where Jason was.

Easter slipped back into the woods and made her way to the other side of the plantation. Every bush, tree, stick, and rock seemed familiar now. When she'd gone around the fields and had reached the slave quarters, she carefully stepped out of the forest. There was less chance someone would discover her there, because everyone was working. There were only some children holding hands and turning around in a circle. They reminded her of Jason. He used to love coming to the plantation to play the ring games with the children there. The old woman who cared for the youngsters while their parents worked in the fields didn't see Easter slip behind a row of cabins and walk quickly toward the big house.

By the position of the sun, Easter figured that it was about two o'clock in the afternoon. She wished that she had some kind of bundle to carry so that she'd look as if she was working. Her eyes darted nervously as she gazed around. She didn't want to run into the master or Mistress Phillips. Several men chopping wood ignored her. Two boys carrying water to the fields glanced her way with uninterested eyes. Two unfamiliar women walked toward her. Each carried a large basket of laundry on her head, while deep in conversation.

Easter averted her face as she hurried past them, but they didn't look in her direction. She sensed a strange quietness about the place. She spotted smoke coming from the kitchen, which was a building adjacent to but separate from the big house. If things were still the same, then her friend Rose and the cook would be in the kitchen preparing the Phillipses' supper. Easter knew that Rose and the cook would help her.

The smell of frying pork drifted out of the slightly open kitchen door. Easter peeped into the room and saw Rose standing over the huge black iron stove, a skillet in her hand.

"Rose, can I come in?" Easter whispered.

Rose turned around quickly, almost dropping the skillet. "Who that?" she asked, squinching her eyes at Easter.

"Rose? It's me. Easter."

"Easter?" Rose's eyes opened wide with surprise. "That really you? I didn't know you. Oh, Easter. I thought I never see you again." She put down the skillet and ran over to her.

Easter cringed shamefully when Rose hugged her. "I a dirty, stinking mess, Rose."

Rose continued to embrace her. "Hush, gal. I smell worse thing than you." Rose was several years older than Easter and had been like a sister to her, always making her feel secure. That hadn't changed.

"I come back for Jason," Easter told her. "You know where he is?" She swayed a little unsteadily on her feet, faint now from fatigue and hunger and fear of Rose's answer.

"He right here with us."

Easter's face spread in a wide smile. "Mistress Jennings didn't give him to Missy Holmes?"

"When your master and Mistress Jennings leave for the West, they sell Jason to Mistress Phillips. I hear Mistress Phillips pay one hundred dollars for him. And I hear Mistress Jennings wanted to take Jason with her, but your old master sell every living and breathing and growing thing, including Jason. Your old master lose a lot of money when you and Obi run."

"Good," Easter said. "He wasn't suppose to be ownin' us in the first place."

Rose led Easter to a chair in front of a large oak table. "Well, Jason is Mistress Phillips's special servant now."

"What you mean?"

"Just what I say—he her special servant. Wear a fancy suit and has nothing to do with the rest of us."

"He act different then?"

"Everything different, Easter." Rose tried to brush a smudge off Easter's nose. "You hungry and need to wash. I get the tub and draw you some water and give you something to eat. Then I tell you everything that happen."

The worry lines creased Easter's forehead. "I don't want anyone to find me here."

"No one come in this kitchen 'less I invite them in," Rose said as she went toward the door. "Mistress is takin' her afternoon rest. I keep things the way the cook use to keep them." Her round eyes clouded.

Easter scanned the kitchen. "That's what's different in here. What happen to the cook?"

"She die, not long after you leave," Rose answered, her voice cracking slightly. Easter felt a lump rising in her own throat, as she remembered how she and Rose used to spend hours and days helping the cook prepare food for the Phillips family on special occasions, how they'd have the kitchen smelling of pies and puddings and candied yams.

Rose brushed her hands quickly across her face. "I miss her," she said.

"So you the cook now?"

Rose nodded. "Yes. I the boss over these pot and pan. I get one of them children out of the yard to fill the tub with water, and you can clean yourself." She called several children to bring her the tin tub out of the woodshed and fill it with water from a barrel outside the door. Easter got up and stood by the pantry closet. If someone came in the kitchen, she'd duck inside.

Rose dragged the tub inside. "Don't look so worried. Nobody come in here." She handed Easter a cake of homemade soap and a clean rag. Easter took off her filthy clothes and slid into the clear water. Rose held up the torn and filthy shirt and pants and wrinkled her nose. "Think we better burn these before mushrooms sprout out of them."

Easter closed her eyes as she soaked. "This better than peach cobbler or sweet potato pie or any good thing to eat."

Rose chuckled. "You must be hungry."

While Easter bathed and Rose cooked, Easter told her everything that had happened to her and Obi. When she finished her bath, Rose brought her a plain homespun dress and a hairbrush. Easter brushed her thick hair, enjoying the feel of the stiff bristles on her clean scalp.

"Now, I see it's my Easter." Rose smiled. Her deep dimples appeared in her round face. Easter felt even more tired after the bath. But she was also hungry. Rose gave her a plate of rice and greens cooked with ham.

"Food kind of scarce because of this war. Mistress always feedin' them soldiers. She never did give the field hands too much ration. Only reason me and the cook ate good was because we work in the kitchen."

Easter wiped her mouth. "This like a feast after eatin' nothing but pork fat and hardtack."

Rose grimaced. "Sound like something that put a hole in your stomach. What's hardtack?"

"Biscuits the soldiers make."

Easter dozed off at the table while waiting for Rose to finish serving dinner to Mistress Phillips. Rose shook her gently when she returned to the kitchen. "Easter, you sleep in the shed with me. I come back later to finish cleaning and to . . ." Her voice trailed off.

"To what?" Easter asked.

"Nothing," she answered quickly, wrapping her plump arm around Easter's shoulders. "You don't know how happy I am to see you."

"Rose, I happy to see you too, and I want to see Jason."

"Let's go to the shed, and I give you the news."

It was dusk when they left the kitchen and walked toward the tiny shed where Rose slept. A black couple strolled from the slave quarters past the big house to the gate of the plantation. That struck Easter as unusual. She remembered that there used to be a curfew, and no one could walk toward the gate without being stopped. *Maybe they have a pass to go somewhere,* she told herself.

When she and Rose reached the shed, Rose lit a candle. A lumpy old horsehair mattress covered with a patchwork quilt lay on the floor. A stool standing next to the mattress and a small scratched table were the only furniture in the room. A red and white gingham dress hung on a peg, and one set of underclothes was neatly folded on the table.

Rose and Easter sat on the mattress. "There be a lot of change since you an' Obi run away. Girl, I pray Master Jennings and his brother Wilson don't find you. Wilson so angry at how you two get away he say he goin' to kill Obi. Master Jennings say no, he ain't lettin' Wilson kill two thousand dollars. They look for you all up and down the countryside. Then they sell the farm and leave for the West."

"How you know all that they say?" Easter asked. She knew that Rose liked a good story and often added her own little touches to the telling.

"Rayford tell me. He overhear Master Phillips talking about it." Rose gazed at her worn slippers. "You remember Rayford?"

Easter nodded. How could she forget Rayford, with his sparkling white shirt and pants that made his smooth black face look like polished ebony; Rayford, who stood as stiff and straight as Master Phillips; Rayford, who had secretly learned how to read and write. He had been Master Phillips's proud personal servant. Some of the other blacks on the plantation called him Massa Rayford.

Easter knew something else about Rayford. "Rose, I tell you a secret, but you promise not to say anything."

Rose moved closer to her. "Lip tight like a clam," she said.

"The night me and Obi run, it was Rayford who help us. He and some of the people here is hidin' guns and knives in coffins."

Rose laughed. "I know about that, Easter. I been to one of them fake funerals. Everything change all at once. Master Phillips take sick and die, then all we hear is that the Yankee is comin' to free us, and the people run away from this place like mouse runnin' from cat."

"I could tell things was different around here, Rose. Where they run to?"

"Some stay in the swamp and the woods. Some get caught by the patterollers—they in the prison. Most we never see again. That's when Master get sick, when all his property run away." Rose lowered her voice to barely a whisper. "Mistress plannin' to move the rest of us to Texas till the war over. But some of us ain't going with her. That's why Rayford an' them been hidin' guns an' knives—so we can protect ourselves when we leave here." Her round eyes were frightened and excited at the same time. "I know I could trust you with this news, Easter."

Easter nodded. "Where you runnin' to?"

"Rayford and some of the other men have it all plan. Rayford been sneakin' and readin' the paper and he know everything that's happenin' with this war. Yankee take over the Sea Islands and that's where we goin'. You free if you get where them Yankee is."

Easter grabbed Rose by the shoulders. "That's where I want to go, to the Sea Islands! That's where Obi is!" Her eyes shone with hope and excitement as she smiled. "I get Jason and we come with you."

"Well, we wasn't plannin' on takin' Jason. He stayin' here in his fancy clothes."

Easter's smile vanished and the creases appeared on her forehead. "I come back for Jason, to take him to the islands with me."

"I sure Rayford won't mind you comin', Easter. Jason probably won't want to leave here anyway."

"He'll come with me. I find my way back to the coast, just like I find my way here. But I ain't leavin' without Jason this time."

"He won't go with you, Easter," Rose insisted.

"Where is he now?"

"In the sittin' room with Mistress. He singin' and she bangin' on the piano. That's what they do every evening God send."

Easter stared wistfully at Mariah's rug lying at her feet. "Jason always love to sing." Her head throbbed. "Rose, can't you get him to come see me now?"

"He go right back to Mistress and tell her you here." Rose stood up, looking away from Easter. "I speak to Rayford, but I know what he say."

Easter watched her friend. "What's wrong with your face? Look funny every time you say the man's name."

Rose smiled shyly. "Oh, hush. I just get his supper for him in the evening. Mistress make him the overseer now, since the soldier draft the white overseer. That's why Mistress workin' so hard on Jason. Tryin' to make him a special servant, like Rayford was."

Easter laughed in spite of her aching head. "Jason like Rayford?"

"Stupid, ain't it? Mistress a little touched in the head. 'Specially after Master die and she have to run this place. Is we who really run the plantation."

Rose patted the large, lumpy mattress. "Sleep, Easter. Tomorrow I think of a way to bring Jason to see you. But I afraid he open his big mouth."

"Jason will listen to me. I know him good."

Rose smoothed her dress. "You use to know him good."

CHAPTER
TWO

We felt perfectly justified in undertaking the dangerous and exciting task of "running a thousand miles" in order to obtain those rights which are so vividly set forth in the Declaration.

From "The Escape of William and
Ellen Craft from Slavery"

Easter felt as if she'd just fallen asleep when she found herself being gently shaken. "Someone here to see you," Rose said. Easter's body was still stiff and sore, and for a moment she didn't know where she was. When she opened her eyes fully, though, and saw Jason standing by the door, she jumped out of the bed and ran to him.

He squirmed in her arms, but she didn't notice until he yelled, "You a runaway an' I tellin' Missy."

Rose twisted his arm. "You ain't tellin' nothing."

Easter was too shocked by his accusation and threat to say anything at first. She could only stare in disbelief at his thin legs encased in white stockings, his brass-buckled shoes, and his green velvet britches and vest to match. The ruffles on his fancy white shirt puffed out over his vest.

She recalled how he looked the last time she had seen him, shirttails made out of sacking flapping around his spindly legs. Now he was dressed like a boy in a painting she'd once seen in the Phillipses' drawing room when she was helping the maids clean; the only difference was that the boy in the picture was white.

Easter's eyes narrowed as she put her hands on her hips and brought her face down close to his. "What you say, Jason? You tellin' on me? You ain't happy to see me?"

"I tellin' Missy," he whined, averting his eyes.

"I come back for you like I promised." She reached for him again but he backed away from her grasp.

"You and Obi leave me." He rubbed his snub nose.

"Jason, I try to come for you, but I couldn't. I here now. I could've escape to the Yankee, but I come back here to get you."

"Missy Phillips say Yankee is the devil."

"You believe anything," Rose said angrily.

Jason's eyes became teary, and he rubbed his nose again. "I don't like you, Easter, and I tellin' Missy that you back here to worry me."

Easter's brown eyes took on a glazed expression. "Jason, you know you ought not talk to me that way." She balled her fist. She'd like to pull those fancy britches off him and give him one good spanking.

"You leave me alone. I hate you, and I tellin' Mistress on you too, Rose, if you put a hand to me." He still made no move to leave the shed.

Rose clenched her teeth. "I like to wring your little chicken neck. See what a brat he is, Easter? See what I tell you?"

This wasn't the same Jason Easter had left. This wasn't her Jason. The real boy was hidden somewhere under the velvet and the ruffles. She'd find him. *Ain't come all this way for nothing,* she said to herself, trying to control the urge to box his ears. "Jason, I back now. And me and you is goin' to find Obi. And all of us be together again," she said firmly and slowly. "I been through misery to get back here for your little tail."

"I with Missy now. Don't want to be with you and Obi."

Suddenly Rose grabbed him by the collar. "Jason, you a

lying rascal. You was up and down the road every day lookin' for Easter and Obi. No matter how much Master Jennings yell and Wilson beat you, you still there every day, in good weather and bad."

The tears streamed down his baby-soft brown cheeks. Easter reached out for him. "Jason, I never forget you." She held him, and after a few seconds she felt his arms shyly circle her neck.

"You ain't leavin' me no more?" He sniffled.

"No, Jason. But don't tell nobody I here. Not even Mistress Phillips."

He nodded. "But you won't run away from me again?"

"I won't, Jason. I never leave you."

Rose folded her arms. "You go back to Mistress, 'fore she come lookin' after you. And don't say a word about Easter, else you get the whipping of your life. Not even Missy stop me."

"I want to stay with Easter," Jason said, squeezing her neck tighter.

"You a contrary devil," Rose mumbled. "You go on back and I bring you to see her later." She abruptly snatched him by his ruffled collar again. "Now don't you say a word to no one."

He tried to squirm out of her grasp. "Yes, Rose. Won't say nothing." She let him go. He fluffed out his collar and hugged Easter once more before leaving.

Easter beamed at Rose. "He himself now."

"I still don't trust him." Rose handed her a wooden plate with grits and a slice of bacon. "Eat some breakfast."

Easter sat on the stool. "What Rayford say? Can I come with you?"

Rose's eyelids lowered, cloaking her great, dark eyes. "He say yes, but he say Jason your responsibility. If Jason don't act right, then you and him have to leave the group. He also say you was a fool not to escape to the islands when you had the chance."

Easter was relieved. "I make Jason behave. How you gettin' him away from Mistress Phillips?"

"That's easy. Mistress 'sleep by ten o'clock—that's when we takin' off. Jason sleep outside her door in the hallway. I wake him and say I bringin' him to see you like I promise." She picked up two baskets. "Now I takin' you to the plantation jail."

Easter hugged herself in mock fright. "You arrestin' me?"

"The jail been empty since the overseer leave and Master die. We use it for the runaways who need a place to hide and rest."

Easter finished eating and picked up her rug. Rose handed her one of the baskets. "Make it seem like we goin' to the garden—what's left of it. Last week some soldiers come through here and dig up most of the vegetables."

"What happen to the dogs?"

"Been poison," Rose answered simply as she stepped out of the shed ahead of Easter. "Come on, ain't nobody 'round," she said. "Mistress still upstairs. Better hurry, in case that Jason tell."

"He won't, Rose." Easter squinted her eyes at the pleasantly warm morning sun. They hurried past the orchards and the magnolia trees. "Rose, you seem upset, but I know Jason ain't goin' to say anything." She smiled at Rose reassuringly, and her face became as bright as the sun. Her full mouth, the color of ripe plums, framed her straight, ivory-colored teeth. "The day feel nice, don't it, Rosie? Sky blue as a jaybird."

Easter's cheerful mood left when they approached the jail, which was at the far end of the plantation. The whipping post was still in the yard. Rose entered the dark, dampish building first. There was a room upstairs where the female prisoners used to be kept and two rooms downstairs, each containing a large cell. Chains and leg irons lay in the corners of the cells. Only a dull shaft of light seeped in through the small windows.

Easter spread her rug on the floor near the door. Rose

stood over her. "Nobody find you here. If Jason open his mouth, I'll swear he lyin'. This jail is the meeting place for tonight." Rose stared at Easter's bare feet. "I find you some old shoes if I can."

Easter grimaced. "No, shoes seem like they hurt. Bring me some rags and I tie my feet."

The day stretched like years. Rose popped in to see her in the late afternoon, bringing her a slice of bread and a cup of buttermilk. She also brought rags so that Easter could bind her feet. Rose seemed happier than she'd been in the morning. "Jason ain't say nothing yet. Maybe he keepin' his mouth shut," she informed Easter.

Finally the sun set, and every nerve in Easter's body seemed to sense the slightest rustle of a leaf. The songs and cries of birds were replaced by the clicks of the night insects. Easter rolled up her rug and stood waiting by the door of the jail. After what seemed like hours, Rose rushed in, pulling Jason behind her. "Where Easter?" he whispered loudly.

"I here, Jason," she answered, and he wrapped his arms around her waist.

"Where we goin'?" he asked.

"You hush now. You want to be with me?"

"Yes."

"Then be still. We together now. Don't you worry about anything else."

Other people began to slip into the jail, but Easter couldn't tell who they were in the darkness. She could see, however, that the men carried shotguns and rifles and the women held bundles. Easter counted five children, including Jason and an infant girl.

Rayford entered, and at first Easter didn't recognize the figure in a straw hat and overalls with a rifle slung over his shoulder; however, she knew the voice. "It should take us no more than a couple of days to get to the Yankee territory. But we have to be careful. There's bands of robbers, runaway soldiers, and all kinds of people living and fighting in the forest. And they're all hungry. We don't want to lose the little food we have. Now, we have to move fast before Mistress discovers we're gone and calls out the patterollers."

"Long as I have shot and a gun, nobody takin' us. Least not alive," one of the men announced.

Rayford turned to the boys. "You must be quiet and do as we say at all times."

"Easter, where we goin'?" Jason whispered as they left the jail.

"Shush! I tell you later," she answered impatiently.

Several men headed up the procession and the rest were behind, so that the women and children were sheltered in the middle as they disappeared into the woods. Easter was elated and felt as if she were being carried as they hurried along. She and Jason were together and soon they'd be united with Obi.

CHAPTER
THREE

For no man should take me alive; I should fight for my liberty as long as my strength lasted.

Harriet Tubman

Easter stared at the sky, but the stars were hidden under heavy clouds. She squeezed Jason's hand as they stepped over dead branches and twigs.

"I tired," he complained after a while. "Missy be angry with me if she know I out here."

"Those other boys ain't grumbling, Jason. Don't waste your breath talking. Save it for walking."

"I want to rest," he whined.

Easter sighed. "Soon, Jason, soon."

Rose, who walked next to Easter, said, "I know he be like this."

Easter ignored her comment. After walking for three hours, they stopped for a short rest. The children immediately fell asleep. One of the women, Isabel, nursed her infant daughter, Miriam.

When it was time to leave, Easter tried to shake Jason awake. "Come on, Jason." He was as limp as a rag doll when she attempted to pull him up.

Another woman was having the same problem with her son. "David, get up," she ordered in a loud whisper. The boy didn't stir. "These children too tired to move," the woman told Rayford.

Rayford tried to wake one of the boys up. "We have to carry them," he said.

Two of the boys were as small as Jason, and could be carried; however, one boy was a large twelve-year-old.

"This Goliath here have to walk on his own," the boy's father said, pulling him up.

They took off again, with Jason and the other two boys being carried piggyback by three of the men. The group stopped one more time when Isabel had to nurse Miriam again.

They continued walking, the men breathing heavily under the weight of the children, until the cry of birds announced a new morning.

Soon they found a spot thick with grass and brush. Sheltering low-hanging branches and vines intertwined like the rugs and baskets Easter and Mariah used to weave. Easter spread her rug on the ground. The man who had carried Jason placed him gently on it, and she lay next to the boy, cradling him in her arms.

Easter woke in the afternoon to the cries of Miriam. She watched Isabel and several of the women trying to quiet her down. For the first time she got to really see her companions and learn their names.

Virginia, George, and their three sons, David, Isaiah and Nathan, were one family; Isabel, Paul, and daughter, Miriam were another family. Besides Rayford, there were three single men—Julius, Samuel, and Elias—and Melissa and Sarah, two middle-age women who were field hands, like the men.

The two women sat together eating bread. Jason slept. David and Isaiah rubbed their eyes, seeming confused. Their bigger brother, Nathan, still slept, snoring loudly. Since Rose had had access to the kitchen, she'd brought most of the food: sweet potatoes, beef jerky, and bread. She passed around bread and sweet potatoes. "Don't y'all go eatin' everything this morning," she warned as she watched Julius gobble down a sweet potato. "We have two more days out here."

"That's right," Rayford said as he sat down near Rose.

When Melissa and Sarah finished eating they came over to Rayford. "We ready, Mister Ray," Sarah said.

Mister Ray must be his new nickname, Easter thought.

Rayford pulled two rifles out of his sack and gave them to Melissa and Sarah. "Go by the creek over there," he said, pointing to several cypress trees. Julius and Samuel picked up their shotguns. "You go around that side, a few feet past that large oak," Rayford told them.

Easter turned to Rose. "What're they doin'?" she asked.

Before Rose could answer, Rayford said, "We're all taking turns keeping watch in case someone comes."

"I help too," Easter said, taking the sweet potato Rose handed her. She didn't want him or anyone else to feel that she couldn't be useful too.

His eyes drooped wearily. "Can you shoot?"

"If someone show me how, I can."

"We don't have time to show people how to do things. You just make sure you keep Jason quiet." He glanced at the boy, who was beginning to stir.

"I will," Easter said. Jason opened his bleary eyes. "Morning, Jason. Want some bread?" she asked him.

He nodded and gazed around as he ate. "My feet hurt," he said.

"You don't have on the right clothes. I ask Virginia if them boys have a shirttail or trouser to lend you. And I wrap your feet. Shoes is bad for feet."

He stared at her as if she'd slapped him in the face. "These clothes fine. Can't wear no shirttail. Too big for that, and gentlemen is suppose to wear shoes, Easter."

Easter tried not to laugh at him. "You aint' no man. Shirttail better than them hot britches you wearin' and them shoes that's chokin' your feet."

He took off his shoes and rubbed his toes. "Missy lookin' for me," he whined.

"She lookin' for all of us," Rose snapped as she got up and walked over to Isabel to offer her food. Rayford had finished eating and was fast asleep, using his sack for a pillow and covering his face with his straw hat.

The remainder of the day was spent taking turns keeping watch and resting. Easter was glad that Jason was too weary to complain and whine and make the others angry with both of them.

When patches of a red sky began to show through the tops of the trees, Rayford woke up. "We'll be moving on out soon and—" He stopped abruptly, seeming to listen for something.

Easter thought that she heard the sound of voices. Suddenly, Elias and Samuel came running from the spot where they'd been keeping watch. George and Paul followed.

"Someone is comin'," Elias said in a frightened, hoarse voice.

Easter froze where she was sitting. "What happen, Easter?" Jason asked, his eyes wide with fear.

Rayford and the others woke up those who were sleeping. Easter tried to appear calm for Jason. "It's nothing," she assured him as she stood up.

"Let's go! Keep moving. Everybody take out your guns," Rayford ordered. Easter promised herself that she would learn how to shoot when all of this was over. Easter noticed that Isabel was trembling and the baby was beginning to whimper. Rayford spun around.

"Quiet that baby!"

"I can't, suh," Isabel said pitifully.

"She doin' the best she can, Mister Ray! Babies can't help cryin'," Paul said angrily. Rayford didn't answer him.

I never know Rayford was such a hard man, Easter said to herself.

They moved quickly, getting scratched by the low-hanging branches. Isabel was ahead of her, and Easter was afraid she'd smother Miriam because she held the baby so close to her body. "Let me hold her, Isabel," Easter said, panting as they ran. Jason ran next to her.

Isabel handed her the baby, and Miriam stopped whimpering as she stared curiously at Easter's unfamiliar face. While she ran, Easter brought Miriam's face close to her own and made tiny sounds. Miriam grinned and cooed at Easter. Everyone ran desperately. David stumbled and Virginia quickly snatched him up off the ground. Jason fell next, and Rose scooped him up and held his hand so that Easter could concentrate on keeping Miriam quiet.

No matter how fast they ran, the sound of voices grew nearer. Then, in an instant, the voices took form and surrounded them.

"We'll shoot! Stop!" a man yelled.

They halted, and Easter felt like sobbing as this moment forced her to relive how she and Obi had been captured by Confederate soldiers. Miriam started to whimper again, and Isabel took her and rocked her until she was silent. Easter recognized the Confederate forage cap of the man who spoke. There were three other men with him. All of them had muskets and rifles. One of them carried a shotgun. Easter wasn't sure whether they were really soldiers. One wore a slouch hat, but he carried an army haversack on his back. Another had on a straw hat. The third one was bareheaded, but he wore an army jacket and had a shotgun like the kind every farmer in South Carolina owned.

"Well, look what we found here," the man in the straw hat said.

"You ain't found nothing here," Paul responded slowly and deliberately.

"But trouble," George added.

The man in the forage cap moved in close to George. "Who you think you're talking to?"

George pointed his gun at the man's nose. "Nobody," he said softly.

"Now we know y'all is runaways," the bareheaded fellow said. "Be nice and put down them guns you stole and come with us quietly and there'll be no more trouble." He turned to the other men. "Reckon we could get a nice reward for returning this bunch."

"Only returning there'll be is you returning to the dust after I shoot you," Rayford said.

The man wearing the forage cap reddened like the sky. "You probably ain't had sense enough to put shot in them guns. We'll string you up by your thumbs and make you call us suh like you're suppose to."

Jason hid his face in the folds of Easter's dress. She felt someone stir by her leg and looked down to see Melissa crouched at her feet, her rifle pointed toward the men. They couldn't see her. Easter stared up at the sky, not wanting to draw attention to Melissa. Melissa's face was set hard as granite. Easter prayed that Melissa wouldn't be seen doing whatever it was she was preparing to do.

The veins in Rayford's temple strained at his skin as he yelled. "You better leave us. You ain't taking no one here." Rayford's loud words even made Easter flinch. *He so angry he lose his proper talk,* she said to herself.

"We'll shoot you," the one in the forage cap said, waving his gun menacingly.

"And we'll shoot you back," Rayford answered.

Julius adjusted the butt end of his rifle on his shoulder. "There be more of us than you, and you may shoot one or two of us, but we'll get all of you."

Straw Hat spit on the ground. "Y'all ain't got the nerve to shoot a white man!"

The second the words left the man's mouth, Easter heard the click as Melissa drew back the hammer on her rifle. The straw hat flew straight off the man's head. He looked as if he'd faint. Someone else fired around the men's feet, and the four of them took off. The baby screamed loudly as if she too were ordering them to go.

"We coming back for you with more men," one of them yelled. "Y'all ain't getting away with this."

"Come on," Rayford ordered. "We got to get out of here!"

The children stumbled and tripped, but they kept going. Even Jason didn't whine. Rayford halted everyone when they reached a grove of live oaks draped with moss. They all collapsed on the ground. "We rest here. I don't think they'll be back. If they really had some men to come back with, they wouldn't tell us," Rayford said. "They're probably runaway soldiers themselves. It's too dangerous to keep running while it's still light. Soon as dusk comes, we'll head out again."

Paul put his arm around Melissa. "Melissa, you have eye like eagle. That Rebel's hat flew off his head like duck swooping out of water."

They laughed softly at the memory of it. Jason got up and stood on a log. "I the hat," he said, grinning, and jumped backward off the thick chunk of wood.

Everyone chuckled even more, trying not to laugh too loudly. "Boy, you a silly thing," Easter said.

Rose's dimples were deep as she held her stomach and wiped her eyes. "You a crazy little jack-a-behind," she said. Even Rayford's strained mouth curved into the slightest of smiles.

Easter sat down and leaned against a tree. Jason rested his head on her shoulder. She recalled that when she and Obi had escaped to the coast, someone had been going to take them to the other side of the river, but they had been captured by Confederate soldiers. She felt as if she was repeating her life, except this time she had Jason with her. She looked at them all as they sat quietly waiting for the dark. "It dangerous at the coast," she whispered in a voice small and fearful.

Everyone turned toward her. "We know that," Paul said.

"This the most dangerous thing I ever done," Isabel remarked softly.

Rose clutched her bundle tightly. "Easter already been to the coast," she informed the others.

Rayford rubbed his half-closed eyes. "You should've gone across to the islands when you had the chance."

"Easter come back for me like she promise," Jason piped up.

"Hope you appreciate what she done for you," Virginia said. They all murmured their agreement.

"Easter," Isabel said in her soothing voice. "Tell us what happen to you at the coast."

Easter told her story so softly that only those who listened closely could hear. "You a brave one," Virginia said when Easter had finished. The other women nodded.

Rayford stood up. "Time to leave," he whispered hoarsely. "We'll get to those Sea Islands, because that's what we have the will to do."

"All of us together with one will," Elias added.

They traveled for two more nights, sustaining and supporting each other. Easter was unafraid, now that she felt that she was really part of the group. Only when they arrived at the coast on the third morning did her fears return. She and Obi had been captured, when they'd almost reached their destination. She held Jason's hand tightly.

Rayford stopped where the woods were beginning to thin out into an open area. "You all stay here. Me and Julius will go to the man who is supposed to take people across."

"Mister Ray," George asked as he rubbed and flexed his long legs, "you think you be safe? Better let the rest of us men come with you. Leave the women and children here." He faced the women. "You hear any trouble. You run and hide in these woods."

Easter was relieved when Rayford refused. "No. Only me and Julius. If there's any soldiers or patterollers, we have passes and a good story for them. They'll be suspicious if there's too many of us. If we don't come back in fifteen or twenty minutes, go back over there by those trees." He pointed toward a heavy growth of cypress trees and thick brush. "Wait there for us."

"What if you don't come back?"

"Let Easter make you one of her basket boat and sneak out here at night," Julius joked.

"We'll be back," Rayford said in a confident voice.

Easter sat on the rock-strewn ground, and Rose and Jason sat on either side of her.

"I scared," Jason whimpered quietly.

"Nothing to be scared of, Jason. We almost there." She glanced knowingly at Rose. Rose's big dark eyes looked frightened. Easter couldn't look at her. "You know what the rest of this plan is, Rose?" she asked, staring at the ground.

"Rayford tell me a boatman been taking people over to the Yankee in his flatboat."

"But there's Rebel camps on this side of the river. They shoot at the Yankee boats."

"Well, they ain't no Rebels on this spot, Rayford been told. They may be farther over. The man he seein' was the headman on a big rice plantation on one of them islands. When the Yankee come and take over the Sea Islands, the man come on this side of the river and carry runaways across."

"I hope he there," Easter mumbled.

"Rayford say the man been doin' this since last year."

Easter's eyes took on a faraway expression. "I wonder if I find Obi soon," she said.

Rose shrugged her shoulders. "Rayford tell me there's a lot of islands. You don't know which one Obi's on. The main thing is, when we get to the other side we be free, Easter."

Easter was suddenly startled by footsteps. Rose and Virginia stood up quickly. Melissa drew her rifle.

"It's only just me," Julius announced. "Come on. We got a river to cross."

They rushed out of the woods, following Julius to a weather-beaten shack. Rayford stood outside talking to a small dark man. The river looked like a gray ribbon unraveling in the morning mist. The man smiled as they approached him. "Glad you get here safe. Just in time too. I gettin' ready to carry these people across," he said, nodding toward several other men and women.

Easter looked around nervously as they walked toward the river, afraid to get excited or happy until they were actually on the island. She and Jason held on to each other as the man plied the flatboat across the river. The mist was so thick that she couldn't see the opposite shore. The boatman's voice seemed to float eerily out of the fog and the lapping water as he spoke. "Been takin' people over to the other side since the Yankee come. The runaways call me the Freedom Man. And I call this thing the Freedom Boat."

"What happen when we get to the island?" Paul asked him.

"The Yankee tell you where to go."

Easter had only one question: *Is Obi on the other side?*

CHAPTER

FOUR

We landed under the protection of the Union fleet, and remained there two weeks, when about thirty of us were taken aboard the gunboat P——; and at last, to my unbounded joy, I saw the "Yankee."

Susie King Taylor
Reminiscences of my Life in a Camp with the 33rd United States Colored Troops

"We free," Isabel cried, kissing Miriam.

"We free!" They all shouted as they stepped off the flatboat. The men hid their rifles and shotguns in sacks before leaving the boat. Sarah sank to one knee, head bowed. Easter looked up at the sky. "Thank you, God," she whispered.

On shore, soldiers in strange blue uniforms mingled among what seemed to be hundreds of black people. Easter studied the scene before her: men, women, children, old people, infants—all in a jumbled mass. One elderly man in rags lay lifeless on the ground. A young woman hobbled on crutches and one leg. There were women in finely tailored dresses and hats, and women with their garments in shreds and their heads tied with cloth. There were field hands wearing dirty overalls and torn trousers, and carriage drivers still in their embroidered jackets.

And there were children everywhere. A baby about a year old wandered aimlessly, crying. One little girl about ten kept five younger children in tow while she carried a baby. Easter almost cried as she watched a white-haired old grandmother surrounded by a brood of children stretch her hands to a bewildered-looking young soldier. A tall, stately white woman in a plain black dress walked over to the children and the elderly woman. She seemed out of place among the crowd of fugitives and soldiers.

The new arrivals gazed silently at the scene. Finally Rayford said, "We'd better talk to one of these soldiers and find out where we can settle."

"Where is we, Easter?" Jason asked, looking worried.

"We made it to Yankee territory, Jason. Now we goin' to find Obi."

"There're a lot of islands in this territory. Obi could be on any one of them," Rayford said.

"I go to each one until I find him," Easter replied.

"That might not be possible."

"But if we free, why can't I look for Obi now?"

Rayford started to answer her, but Jason interrupted. "I want to go back home, Easter. Why you bring me here?"

"That's enough," Rayford said to both of them. "We have to find food and shelter, then we worry about finding folks."

"That's right," Paul agreed. "We have to find our new life."

Rayford led them toward two soldiers, who by the gleaming medals on their jackets and by the way they barked orders appeared to be officers.

"Are all of you families?" one of the soldiers asked. "We can't be responsible for the young children."

Easter had trouble understanding his speech. Jason, mouth open slightly and eyes open wide, stared at the man's mouth in fascination.

"Yes sir, we are all family members here," Rayford answered.

"We need laborers to work on one of the cotton plantations. Can you people do that kind of work?"

"Yes," Rayford answered.

The young officer turned to another soldier standing next to him. "They seem healthy and strong. Better than most."

Easter thought that it was pretty rude to talk about people who stood right in front of you. She stared at the shredded rags on her feet and wondered how she'd begin to find Obi in all of this mess and confusion.

"You go to the plantation now," the soldier told them. "Hurry along to that man standing by the wagon over there." He pointed to a young black man standing next to a rickety wagon drawn by two mules. Easter heard Elias whisper to Melissa, "This don't sound like we free. He orderin' us to go."

Rayford shifted from one sore foot to the other. "Sir, do we get pay for our work?"

"Yes. We need laborers to grow the crops on the abandoned plantations."

"That sound better," George mumbled.

"How much money do we get?" Rayford asked.

"That's up to the superintendent of the plantation. He'll tell you. But you will be paid."

Paul, holding Miriam, asked, "We free now?"

"Well, the Rebels can't buy and sell you as long as you're with us. Now, go to those people by that wagon, and you'll be taken to the Williams plantation."

They started to walk away, but Rayford stopped. "Sir, what's the name of this island?"

"Santa Elena," the soldier answered.

Easter wanted to ask how she could get from one island to another in order to find someone, but she couldn't approach these strange-talking white men.

They traveled over sandy roads. The wagon driver worked on the plantation they were going to. "Live on the Williams place all my life," he said. "Lot of our people leave when the Yankee come and free us, but me and my family stay and work for soldier. My pa is Brother Thomas, a preacher man. Glad more people like you folks is comin'. Too much work for the few of us who here on the plantation."

Easter ignored the man's chatter and observed her new surroundings. The most noticeable sensation was the pungent smell of saltwater mixed with the odor of green plants.

Jason noticed it too. "Smell funny 'round here," he exclaimed.

The waxy green leaves of marsh elder and salt myrtle grew out of the sandy soil near the marshes. "This is a watery place," Rose commented.

After riding for about an hour, they crossed a small wooden bridge built over a creek and reached the Williams plantation. The creek ran through the plantation. Easter was surprised at how large the place was—much larger than the Phillips plantation. They passed the dairy, smokehouse, spinning house, and fowl house as they rode toward the family home.

Gates marked the entrance to the plantation. An avenue of live oaks, with Spanish moss hanging like long brown beards, lined the path from the gates to the big house. The house was encircled by a veranda. Magnolia and dogwood trees stood near either side of the house. A group of sturdy cottages sat behind the big house. Farther back from the cottages, near the stables, the slave quarters began, long rows of dilapidated huts facing each other.

Fences for the cattle and other livestock looked like large white circles on the green grass. The vegetable gardens, where the plantation's food was grown, were adjacent to the quarters. Beyond the shacks in the quarters stretched cotton fields, as far as the eye could see. Men and women with long hoes turned over the dirt around the cotton plants.

Instead of a mistress and master, soldiers in blue uniforms and a gray-haired man in a long dark coat sat in the shade of a flower garden. The new laborers left the wagon, and the driver instructed them to present themselves to the gray-haired man. "That's the superintendent," he said, "Mr. Reynolds."

Jason's heels were worn down, the buckles were gone from his shoes, and his white stockings were now charcoal gray. The ruffles on his shirt had been destroyed by a low-hanging branch. He found his voice after a long, wide-eyed silence. "Is they Yankee?" he whispered to Easter.

"Yes, Jason."

"Well, where is they horn?"

The other boys snickered.

"Hush up that foolishness," Rayford ordered.

Jason ignored him. "Missy say Yankee have horn and tail. I know that one in the coat is hidin' the longest tail in the world."

David, Isaiah, and Nathan roared. Their father glared at them, and they stopped laughing. Easter pulled Jason's ear. "This ain't no time for play."

"Sir," Rayford said to Mr. Reynolds, "the soldiers sent us here to work."

The man fingered a set of keys dangling from his belt and ran his fingers through his graying hair. His large watery eyes appeared tired. "This land no longer belongs to the former owners because they are rebelling against the United States government," he said automatically, as if he'd been repeating the same speech for a long time. "If you work this land, then you will have a share in it because you will have helped us in this war effort."

Jason covered his mouth and began to giggle. "The words stuck up in he nose." Isaiah let out one laugh before he was popped on the side of his head by his father.

Rayford glared at Jason. "You mean, if we work here for the government, we get to keep some of the land for ourselves?" he asked.

"That's a good possibility," Mr. Reynolds answered, staring at Rayford closely.

"Well, excuse me, sir," Rayford continued, "but is this a true bargain? We will get this land if we bring in the crop?"

"Yes," Mr. Reynolds snapped impatiently.

"Well, sir, could you write that on a piece of paper?"

There was a gasp among the crowd. *He get whipped now for sure*, Easter thought to herself. She peeped at Rose, who beamed proudly at Rayford.

The man looked as if he was astonished by Rayford's request. "The United States government isn't making contracts with . . . with anyone. You help us, and we'll help you people."

Rayford stared at the man for a moment and then turned to the others. "What do you want to do?" he asked.

"We stay here," Elias said. "At least we get pay." The rest of them agreed.

"Each family gets two and a half acres to till and forty cents a day. You can rent land from us to grow your own vegetables on."

"Suh," Melissa said, "we don't want to work on Sunday."

"I know, I know," Mr. Reynolds said impatiently. "The other people on this plantation already told me that they want Sundays off."

Easter became increasingly disappointed as she walked with the rest to the former slave quarters. This was just another plantation; they'd be spending long hot days in the cotton fields. She came to the island to find Obi, not to pick cotton. When they reached the quarters she saw that the dwellings were crude log huts, even smaller than those on the Phillips plantation.

"Master Reynolds say these last four cabin are for us," George said, surveying the area.

"Why you call the man Master? That's slavery time talk," Julius corrected him. "Call him Mr. Reynolds."

George waved his hand at Julius. "It all the same."

Melissa and Sarah would share a cabin with Easter, Rose, and Jason. The two families each had a cabin, and the single men shared one.

"What kind of freedom is this? I never live in a slave hut," Easter complained.

"Neither did I," Rose said. "I sleep in a shed, and you sleep on Master Jennings's kitchen floor. Least this hut be our own."

"And I slept in the big house. Had my own room in the servant's quarters," Rayford reminded Easter. "And I ain't complaining!" Rayford left them and went with the other men to look at his new home.

"I just glad to have a roof over my head," Sarah said quietly.

But when they opened the cabin door Easter felt like crying. It was worse than she'd thought. "The Jennings kitchen better than this," she moaned.

Jason looked outraged. "This place nasty!" he yelled.

Melissa grimaced. "Come on, Sarah. We go get some water so we can clean that floor." They put their bundles on the floor and left.

"The first thing we have to do is daub those chinks with clay and sweep out this room," Rose mused, scanning the floor and walls. There were two pallets on the floor, three beds hanging on pegs and folded against the wall, a fireplace, and a bench. Easter lay her rug before the fireplace, and Jason immediately sprawled on it and fell asleep.

"I help you clean in here, but me and Jason can't stay long, Rose."

Rose dropped her sacks near Jason's head. "Easter, where you goin'?"

"I have to find Obi."

"That ain't possible. You don't even know where he is. You can't go runnin' all over the place lookin' for somebody with this war goin' on. Never know when there be a battle right here. Don't think them Rebels ain't go try and get these islands back."

Easter crossed her arms defiantly. "I run away from my master and mistress. I run away from the Rebels, and I run again if I have to."

Rose reached into one of her bundles and removed several wooden plates and a small pot. "You can't make things the way *you* want them to be. Obi might not even be thinkin' 'bout you."

Rose's words were like the lash of a whip across Easter's back. Tears welled up in her eyes.

Rayford entered the room. "That place we have is worse than this. We don't have enough beds," he said to Rose.

Rose found a broom near the fireplace and started sweeping around Jason's head. "Easter don't want to stay."

"I have to find Obi," she explained.

"Where will you go? How will you live?"

"That's the same thing I ask," Rose said.

Rayford sat on the bench. "We stay here and work and we'll have something of our own when the war's over. You can look for Obi when the war ends."

"When it be over?" she asked. He didn't answer her.

"You act like you ain't got all your senses!" Rose shouted, pulling out her quilt and shaking it furiously.

"Rose is right. You were lucky before. How you and that boy getting from island to island? Who's going to protect you? Him?" Rayford asked, pointing to the sleeping Jason.

"God protect me," Easter replied.

"God protect those who know how to protect themselves," Rayford muttered.

"Give me one of them guns. I learn how to shoot, then I protected."

"I ain't giving you anything. You better stay with us."

"Easter, don't be so hardhead," Rose said.

Why can't they understand, Easter thought to herself.

"After you find Obi, then what? What you think Obi doin' if he still alive? Workin' on a plantation!" Rose said.

"These people are renting us land and paying us to work. We could be like real men and women now. Have our own land, house, and family." Rayford's dark eyes seemed to peer inside of her. She turned away from him.

"I don't care about no house and land. You mean this

kind of house?" She stretched her arm toward the wall, with its big chinks between the logs. "And pickin' cotton in a burning field? I want a house like Missy Phillips have. I never see Missy pickin' no cotton, and she be free."

Rayford spun her around. "You're a child, or else you'd understand. You can leave if you want. I ain't your father or your master, so I can't stop you. But I ain't helping you do something stupid." He put his hand on Rose's arm. "We meeting tonight with the other people who live here so we can all get to know one another."

Rayford walked out, and Rose and Easter faced each other. Easter didn't want Rose to be angry with her. She loved Rose. But Rose couldn't seem to understand how she felt. All Easter could say was, "I help you clean," as she picked up the bundles from the floor and placed them on the bench so that she could sweep thoroughly.

That evening, when Rose, Melissa, and Sarah left for the meeting, Easter lay down on the pallet. For the first time she did something that she hadn't done for many years. She tried to imagine her mother. Someone holding her and playing with her, the way she'd watched Isabel play with Miriam. But the only image that came to her was her former mistress, who had never played with her.

And now she had nobody but herself. But did she own herself? She recalled Mariah's last words to her, and she talked to God. *Do I own myself?* she asked. She felt like nobody. Maybe she should have stayed with Mariah and Gabriel. Jason had been happy with his Missy and his fancy clothes; maybe she should never have gone back to the plantation for him.

The next morning the sound of the wake-up horn startled her. She rubbed her eyes and shook Jason. He rose with his usual whine. Rose was already up and ready for work. She wore a straw hat and a rough apron over her dress.

"Rose, you a cook. How you goin' to work in the field?"

"I learn. I gettin' pay for this. Better fix yourself some grits 'fore you leave," she said curtly and left the room.

When Jason and Easter got outside, they saw men and women walking to the fields. Some of them nodded in their direction, but Easter ignored them. She saw Rayford leaving his hut, but she made believe that she didn't see him. She walked toward the big house, away from the fields. She would ask one of the soldiers directions to other plantations and other islands so that she could begin her search.

"Now where we goin', Easter?" Jason limped like an old man with bad feet.

"To Obi." She wasn't in the mood for a lot of talk this morning.

When she walked up to the man in the long coat, the same dignified white woman she had seen among the refugees the day before stood next to Mr. Reynolds. The woman fanned herself quickly as she talked in that fast, funny Yankee way. Several black children in shirttails stood quietly by her side. Jason's attention was drawn to the other children.

"Oh, good." The woman smiled. "Here are two more." She stared at Jason's torn ruffles and ruined velvet britches.

"Are you orphans?"

Easter was bewildered. "What, Mistress?"

The woman questioned Mr. Reynolds. "Are they orphans? We have room for a few more."

Easter addressed the man, since she had no idea what the woman was talking about. "Excuse me, suh, but where is—"

The woman interrupted her. "Do you have a mother and a father?" the woman asked, bending slightly in Easter's direction.

Easter understood that. "No, Mistress." She wondered why the woman was asking her these questions.

The woman turned to Mr. Reynolds. "These two should come with me. I like to keep sisters and brothers together when possible."

Easter's heart raced. What was this woman talking about? "Suh, I want to know how to—"

The woman interrupted her again. "How would you like to come north with me and attend our school for colored orphans?"

Easter frowned as she tried to understand the woman's speech.

"Oh no, Mistress." She pulled Jason closer to her.

"You can't stay here if you have no family to care for you," Mr. Reynolds said.

"I don't want to stay here, suh."

She realized that they did not understand her. The man waved his hand at them. "Take these two."

Worry lines appeared on Easter's forehead, and her full lips trembled. "No. Don't take us nowhere, Mistress. Thought we was free now."

Mr. Reynolds ran his fingers through his hair. "You'll go wherever we send you. We can't have children running wild. You have to go with this lady from the missionary society."

"I not a child," Easter protested. She felt the presence of someone behind her. She turned around and stared up at Rayford's face.

"Sir, this is my niece and nephew. I'll take care of them," Rayford said.

The woman addressed him. "You seem intelligent. Don't you think it's a wonderful chance for them to learn how to read and write?"

"They don't want to go north. I'll take care of them and teach them how to read and write."

The woman looked shocked. "You're literate?"

"Yes, ma'am," he said.

She stared at Easter. "Do you want to stay here with your uncle?"

"Yes, Mistress. We love him very much," Easter added for good measure. Jason started to say something, but she clamped her hand over his mouth. She knew that she should thank Rayford, but she couldn't look at him as they walked toward the huts.

"Now you heard the man, Easter. He gave me responsibility for you and Jason, and I say that you and he are going to the field like the rest of us." He stared at Jason. "I have to get you some work clothes."

"I could tote water in these clothes," Jason said, pulling at the ruffles that were hanging off his shirt.

"You're too old for toting water. You're helping Easter and Rose hoe the field."

Jason's bottom lip slid out in a pout. "Missy say I special an' shouldn't work in no field."

"Missy? I don't see any Missy around here," Rayford teased. Easter stared at the field, eyes blurred with tears. "No use crying, Easter. This is the way things are," he said with finality.

"You tell the lady you teachin' me how to read and write. You mean that?" she asked, wiping her eyes.

"I'll teach you—after you finish your task in the field."

"I learn how to write, then I write myself a pass to leave here."

Rayford threw his head back and laughed. "That's slavery time. You're free now. Who're you going to show a pass to? The soldiers? They're going to stop firing at each other and let you pass with your pass? Mr. Reynolds ain't paying passes no mind. He'll send you with some other group of motherless children. Put leaving here out of your mind. You're not going anywhere anytime soon."

CHAPTER
FIVE

The dream of my life is not yet realized. I do not sit with my children in a home of my own.

Harriet Jacobs
Incidents in the Life of a Slave Girl

"Easter, let's go back to Missy," Jason whined as they neared Rayford's cabin.

She snatched what was left of his ruffles, turned him around and spanked him. "Jason, I your Missy now. Don't—want—to—hear—nothin' else about Missy." She punctuated each word with a whack.

"You should've done that a long time ago," Rayford muttered.

When she released him, Jason dashed toward the woods. Easter started to follow, but Rayford grabbed her arm. "He'll be back."

"Suppose he try and get to his Missy?"

Rayford smiled. "He'll have to swim. He's not going to walk in those woods by himself. The only other way out is past the missionary lady. He's probably hiding behind one of those trees and watching us talking."

Rayford entered his hut and returned with a pair of old trousers and a piece of rope. "He can wear these." He handed Easter the pants and rope. He also gave her a long-

44

handled hoe. "Julius will show you how to use this. He's in the field with Rose now."

Easter dug her bare feet into the dusty lane and tried to thank Rayford for helping her, but she couldn't get the words out. How could she be thankful about staying on the plantation and having to work in the fields? She walked back to her hut and left the trousers on Jason's pallet.

On her way to the fields she spotted a flock of robins flying toward the pines, away from the plantation. She wished she was as free as they were.

When she reached the field, Julius was showing Rose how to loosen the ground and chop away the marsh grass growing around the cotton plants. He bowed to Easter as she neared them. "Good morning, Miss Easter." He smiled, tipping his battered straw hat. Easter saw nothing to smile about. Her face was as long as the rows of cotton plants as she followed his instructions. The sun beat relentlessly on her head, and she wished that she had her straw hat.

They worked steadily, but Easter couldn't stop looking toward the woods to see whether Jason would appear. "Well, ladies," Julius said, "I think you know what to do. Just don't uproot the plant." He grinned broadly, especially at Easter, showing almost perfectly straight white teeth. Then he left to work in his own field.

Easter felt Rose's eyes on her. "Why you didn't leave?" Rose asked.

Easter carefully loosened the dirt. Looking at the plant and not at Rose's probing eyes, she told her what had happened.

At first, Rose was silent. Then a low giggle escaped her mouth. "So Uncle Ray save you from the missionary lady. I hear it cold up in the North. Oh, Lord, Easter, wish I could've been there to see it." Rose bent down and pulled out the grasses growing around the plant. "Where the brat? Did he go north with Missy Missionary?" She imitated Jason's whine.

"I give him one good spanking, and he run and hide in the woods."

Rose laughed so hard and loud that the other hands looked at her and chuckled too.

Rose's laughter was contagious. Easter was surprised at herself for smiling in a cotton field. The sun burned hotter as the morning dragged on. She tried to throw thoughts out of her mind like a farmer dumping hay out of a wagon.

Stopping for a moment, Easter scanned the edge of the woods for Jason. She noticed that very young children were playing near the fields while the older children carried water and some helped with the hoeing. Easter watched Isabel walk toward a tiny bundle lying on the ground and realized that the bundle was Miriam. Another woman carried her child, about three months old, tied to her back as she worked.

Easter shaded her eyes and gazed toward the cabins. A small, brown figure walked slowly toward the fields. As it drew closer, she recognized Jason. He'd snuck back into the cabin and put on the old trousers, tying the rope around his waist to hold them up. He still wore his ruffled shirt.

"I sorry I hit you," she told him when he walked over to her. He didn't respond.

"Why you keep that shirt on?" she tried again.

"Missy say gentlemen always wear shirt." He looked down at his feet.

Easter snatched him by his arm. "I don't want to hear bout no Missy!"

He jerked away from her, listening in silence as she showed him how to hoe the ground.

They dragged wearily back to their huts when the sun set. Easter thought that her back was broken. Suddenly Jason stopped walking, pulled off his broken-down shoes, and flung them into a bush.

When they reached their cabin, Melissa said, "Better fix something to eat. I starvin'." She rummaged through a sack hanging near the fireplace. "Let's see, the Yankee give us two pound of rice and some salt pork. Guess we could—"

Sarah pulled her arm. "Look at them," she said, pointing to Easter, Jason, and Rose. They'd collapsed, drunk from exhaustion, on the bench. Jason lay his head on Easter's lap. "I too tired to eat, Melissa," Easter moaned.

"Field work is terrible when you not use to it. But you'll get use to it. You'll always be tired, but not too tired to eat."

I never get use to this, Easter told herself as she rubbed her back. *And I figurin' a way to leave.*

At the end of the week all of them reported to Mr. Reynolds's assistant for their pay. Easter, unable to count, stared at the two coins in her hands.

"That's two dollars," Julius said, peeping over her shoulder as they left the large shed where the farm tools were kept.

She frowned. "Is it much?"

"If you keep savin' these dollars, it can be a lot." Julius placed his two silver dollars in a small leather pouch.

"What do I get?" Jason asked, running up to Easter.

"If you work hard, I give you one of these." She held up a silver dollar.

They walked past the stables. Julius rubbed Jason's head. "Well, little fella, what you goin' to buy with one whole dollar?"

"A new shirt, new shoes, and new britches."

"Well, Miss Easter, I think you have to give this boy more money."

"He have to work harder than he work this week."

"What're you goin' to do with your money?" Julius asked Easter.

She shrugged her shoulders, wishing he'd stop asking her so many questions. She had no idea what she would do with the money, except save it. She figured she'd need money when she left the plantation.

Before going to sleep that night, Easter tore the ruffles

completely off Jason's shirt, and taking two pieces of the material, she wrapped a coin in each. "Half for me and half for you," she told Jason. His tired eyes managed to brighten a bit.

"If I work in the field, I get one dollar each week?" he asked.

"Yes, but you have to really work, Jason. Not play."

She tore the sleeves off his shirt and held it up. "I'll wash this shirt good, and it look like new. Now it's right for working in the field." But Jason was fast asleep and didn't see his altered shirt.

The next day was Sunday. Rose, wearing her red and white gingham dress, stood over Easter, who was just waking up. "The people have a Sunday church service, and they invite all of us. Why don't you come?" Rose said.

Easter sat up, rubbing her eyes. "I want to sleep."

"I tired and sore too, but I goin'."

Easter lay back down. "I too tired, Rose."

Rose left. Easter had begun to drift off to sleep again when she heard sounds. At first she thought that someone was crying. She listened harder and realized that it was singing—voices rising and falling and rolling toward her in waves. Jason stirred. "We goin' in the field today?" he asked.

Easter stretched. "No. It Sunday."

"See, if I was with Missy, she give me a special Sunday morning breakfast and then we sing and then—"

"What I tell you about that Missy talk? You know what happen the last time you tell me about Missy."

"Who's singin'?" Jason asked, getting up from the pallet.

"People here havin' church, I guess."

"What they singin'?" He walked to the door and peeped out. Easter got up and put on her dress over her long slip. "Let's go an' hear the singin', Easter," Jason said.

"I don't want to."

"Can I go?"

"Yes." She doused her face with water from the bucket hanging by the fireplace.

"Come with me."

"I told you, I don't want to."

"Then I stay here with you and talk about how I want to see Missy." He took his britches and shirt off the peg. "What happen to my shirt?"

"I fix it for you. And why you puttin' on them dirty britches?"

"Missy say you have to dress for church."

"Them people down in the woods. That's no real church."

He peeped at Easter with a mischievious gleam in his eyes. "If I was with Missy, we go to a real church and—"

She reached for him, but he scooted out of the cabin. As he raced toward the singing, Easter followed him, going behind the stables toward a cluster of pine trees. It seemed as if all of the blacks on the plantation were there. Jason sat down on the ground, squeezing himself between David and Isaiah. Some of the people sat on logs and fallen tree trunks, and others sat on the pine-carpeted ground. Easter sat behind everyone else. This was the first time Easter had seen all of the other workers on the plantation. Altogether there were about fifty men, women, and children.

A heavyset dark man stood up before the group and said a prayer. Easter sent up her own prayer—that she and Jason be reunited with Obi. They sang again:

> Come by here, my Lord, come by here
> Come by here, my Lord, come by here
> Come by here, my Lord, come by here
> Oh, Lord, come by here
>
> Someone's praying, Lord, come by here
> Someone's praying, Lord, come by here
> Someone's praying, Lord, come by here
> Oh, Lord, come by here.

The same man addressed the group after singing. "We welcome the new people among us. If we work together, we'll move ahead. You know five lions hunting together catch more possum than one lion hunting he own supper."

"Brother Thomas, don't start preachin' all over again," a woman called out.

Thomas, ignoring her, continued. "I think since this here Superintendent Reynolds is runnin' this plantation that when we have problems we pick three or four men to be the ones to tell him the complaints. People been grumblin' about this and that. So now if you have problems, you come to one of these men and they speak to Mr. Reynolds."

Melissa stood up. "Tell me, mister, who will pick these men to talk for us?"

Brother Thomas wiped his sweating forehead with a handkerchief. "You pick them. You new people choose two men from your group, and we who've been living here choose two men." His broad face spread into a wide smile. "The people who've always lived here, now, who do you want to pick?"

"Thomas, you put your big self up there, may as well stay," one of the men told him.

Everyone laughed.

"Since you all insist that I be the one, then I the one," he said.

A pretty young woman holding a baby stood up. "I pick Elijah."

"That's your husband," another woman responded.

"That's why I pick him."

"Elijah, you the second one." Brother Thomas motioned for the man to join him.

Julius slipped next to Easter. "Who you pickin' from our group?"

He startled her, and she moved a little away from him. "What difference it make? What all this mean anyway?"

"Something we never had before. I had to go beg to Master Phillips for anything I got."

Easter looked bored. "Now you beg to Yankee master."

"So, who you pickin'?"

"No one."

Rose called out Rayford's name, and everyone who came from the Phillips plantation clapped.

"Miss Easter, who else you pickin'?" Julius nudged her arm with his elbow.

He worrisome as Jason, she thought to herself. "I pick you so you can stand up there with them other men and leave me be."

Paul's name was called, and she watched him join the other three men. Julius seemed hurt by her remark. "I didn't mean to worry you." His sharp, high cheekbones and dark skin reminded her of Mariah. She felt a twinge of guilt about being rude, but she didn't feel like talking. She wanted to listen to the others.

"Now we one people. No more 'new people' and 'people who already been here.' " Brother Thomas spread his arms. "We the people of the Williams plantation."

The young woman who'd voted for her husband stood up. "We women who have babies can't tend to the children and go in the field too. We need an old nurse to care for the children like we use to have."

Another woman joined her. "Cookin' in the morning make me get in them field too late, then I don't finish my task and earn my full money. We need a plantation cook."

A man interrupted the women. "We need to build a church and a school for these children. I hear the Yankee sendin' teachers to learn the children on the plantations."

"I want to learn how to read and write too," someone else shouted.

Brother Thomas held his hands up. "Not all at once, and not now. We have a meeting every Saturday afternoon and—"

A woman burst in on his comments. "We have chores

then. After church is the best time to have a meeting."
The other women also demanded that meetings be held on
Sundays when church ended. The men agreed.

Easter stood up as people continued to discuss, argue,
laugh, and chat. The children began to wander away from
the adults and play nearby. Isaiah and Nathan giggled as
Jason performed his hat-shot-off-the-head imitation. Easter
walked away from the grove toward the cabins but changed
her mind about going inside. She had to plan what she
would do next. The idea of running away and searching the
island alone frightened her, even though she talked brave
in front of Rose, but what else could she do? If she ran this
time, at least she'd have Jason with her. Yet where would
they look for Obi? How would they eat? Where would they
sleep? And if Obi wasn't on this island, how would they
get to the other islands?

Her questions left her feeling helpless as she wandered
toward the garden near the big house. She knew that she
couldn't leave tomorrow or the next day, but she *would
leave.* She'd learn her way around the island first and maybe
even begin to build a basket boat to carry her and Jason to
the other islands. She wondered whether there were missionary ladies on all of the islands. She and Jason would
have to be careful of them. They'd also have to avoid
Yankee soldiers. As far as Easter could tell, they were
making people work in the fields. She wondered what the
soldier at the shore would have said to Rayford if Rayford
had said that he didn't do field work. *Probably send us back
across the river.*

Easter found herself in the middle of the flower garden
and started to return to the huts. The garden was for the
pleasure of the family who owned the plantation. She
almost laughed at herself as she remembered that there was
no master or mistress, and on closer inspection she saw
that there were more weeds than flowers.

Stretching out on her back, Easter watched the fat white
clouds and listened to the sounds of squealing and giggling

children. A child of about three or four ran behind two girls just a few years older. Easter had seen them with their mothers that morning.

The bigger girls were trying to catch butterflies. Easter propped herself on her elbows and watched them. As she listened to their joyous laughter, her mind drifted to the woman who complained about having no nurse for the babies. She sat up quickly as if she'd been snatched off the ground. *I be the nurse,* she said to herself. Since she hadn't figured out a way to leave, at least she wouldn't have to work in the fields while she was there.

The idea excited her so much that she ran up to the children as they tried to corner a large monarch butterfly.

The youngest child stared at Easter and pointed to the butterfly.

"I catch it for you," Easter whispered. "Now you all be quiet." She put her index finger to her lips. The children's eyes glistened with admiration as they watched her tiptoe toward the butterfly hovering over a cluster of daisies. Easter caught it. She knelt down, cupping her hands so that the children could see the trapped, fluttering insect.

"It pretty," one of the girls murmured.

"Now we have to let it go," Easter told them after each child took a turn looking at it.

"Why, miss? We want to keep it."

"Keep it," the youngest one repeated.

"Can't do that. He want to go home. Maybe he have a wife and baby waitin'."

Easter uncupped her hands, releasing the butterfly. She waved good-bye to the children. "I have to go now." She was anxious to tell Rose her idea.

"Miss, why you have to go?" one of the girls asked. "Play with us."

"I'll play with you again. But not now." She gently patted the littlest girl's soft face.

Rose was talking to Rayford, as the crowd began to disperse. "Rayford," Easter called, "I want to talk to you. I have an idea," she announced excitedly. "Instead of me goin' in the field, I take care of the young children, since there's no nurse to tend them while their mothers work."

Rayford and Rose stared at her with surprised looks on their faces. "Who'll help me in the field?" Rose asked.

"Jason do my part."

"That lazy rascal?" Rose rolled her eyes toward the sky.

"How're you going to earn money?" Rayford asked.

"Since I the nurse, that's my job. The Yankee pay me forty cents a day to take care of them babies."

"They're not going to pay you to mind babies," Rayford said. "They're paying you to do one thing—pick cotton."

CHAPTER
SIX

To every realm shall peace her charms display,
And heavenly freedom spread her golden ray.

Phyllis Wheatley

June 1862

The next day Easter continued to talk to Rose about her plan to care for the young children. "Rose, I see to it that Jason do his part. What he don't do I finish on Saturdays."

Jason was on the other side of the field, working steadily. Easter had promised him the whole two dollars if he did a good job of helping Rose.

"But you don't want to work in the field."

Easter squinted at the sun. "One day's not as bad as six."

Rose straightened up, rubbing her back. "Rayford say he'll ask Mr. Reynolds about you takin' care of the babies. He let you know what Mr. Reynolds say."

"I hope Mr. Reynolds say yes."

Rose bent down to her work again. "I think Rayford was right. They only payin' us to grow the cotton."

Easter pulled away the grass and weeds around a cotton plant. "Oh, Rose, you always think Rayford is right."

"Well, he usually is."

Easter felt hopeful, and she wasn't going to let Rose discourage her. The women needed someone to take care of the younger children during the day; she could do the job as well as anyone. First she'd get out of the fields, and next she'd leave the plantation altogether.

As she helped Rose prepare supper that evening, she couldn't wait for Rayford to come in with the news. She practically pounced on him when he entered the cabin. "What Mr. Reynolds say?"

Rayford sat wearily on the bench. "He said that we have to make our own arrangements for taking care of the children. He's paying us to bring the cotton crop in."

Easter was speechless for a moment. She felt Rose's eyes on her. She'd been so sure he'd say yes. "They need someone to take care of the children," she almost shouted.

Melissa handed her a plate. "No need to upset yourself, Easter. That's an old woman's plantation job."

Rayford took up his rice and began to talk to Rose about something else. Easter and Jason sat together on the grass rug. The others sat on the bench. Easter stared at her plate of cow peas, rice, and cornbread.

"You better eat, 'fore you get sick," Sarah told her.

The chinks in the logs had been filled in with clay and the floor had been cleaned. The fireplace was scoured so that it almost shone. Rose's gingham dress hung on a peg, as it had done in her shed on the Phillips plantation. The room was as clean as they could make it. Easter listened in angry silence as Rose talked.

"Paul say he goin' to make us a table and one more bench when he finish the chairs he makin' for George and Virginia." She scooped up a spoonful of rice. "He say he have orders for tables and benches for over half the people here. Some of them payin' him money. Some givin' him a chicken or vegetables from their garden."

Melissa picked up a piece of cornbread. "We have to make us some quilts before the cold weather hit this piece of a hut."

Easter heard their talk as if from a distance. Jason had finished eating. He lay with his head in her lap, and as usual he'd fallen asleep. Then Sarah said something about the meeting on Sunday, and Easter listened. Another idea began to form. She'd go to the meeting and ask the women to let her take care of their children. They could pay her, just as Paul was being paid for his carpentry.

Easter woke Jason and led him to his pallet. She kept her new idea to herself.

Between the scorching sun and keeping after Jason to do his work, Easter was worn out by the end of the week. A few times she was tempted to tell Rose about her new plan, but she remained silent.

When Sunday arrived, she started getting nervous about speaking at the meeting. Jason had pestered her into washing his britches and mending and washing his torn vest. He insisted on wearing the altered ruffled shirt. She'd also washed and mended her one dress.

Jason seemed to be carried somewhere else by the singing. His high, clear voice rang out. All Easter could think about was the meeting that was to follow their church service. Even though she didn't know what the proper amount of time for praying was, she believed that Brother Thomas prayed the longest prayer she'd ever heard. *Even God stop listenin' after all this time,* she thought. Eventually, a man shouted, "Amen, Brother. Save some for next Sunday."

A big chorus of amens rose up to the pines. Brother Thomas wiped his forehead and pulled on the straps of his overalls. "It mighty rude to interrupt a man who speakin' to his God. Let the meeting begin, then."

Rayford, Paul, and Elijah joined Thomas in front of the group. Easter listened attentively as people made their complaints and comments about what they wanted. She waited patiently for the right moment to speak.

"Mr. Reynolds is leavin' to run another plantation," Thomas announced.

"Who they bringin' in here to boss us?" an old man asked.

"No one," Thomas answered. "We tell him we can run

this place. We been runnin' it. Yankee don't know nothing about growin' cotton. We tell him we work hard and do the job like we know how to do it, as long as he don't bring no boss man over us." Everyone was pleased.

Easter sighed. *I never get a chance to speak,* she said to herself.

Brother Thomas continued. "We tell Mr. Reynolds that we pick our own overseer from among us. And another thing, we ask him about the land again, and he say that we get the same amount of land we work."

There was a lengthy debate over who should be chosen. Finally Rayford was picked. "Now Mr. Ray will be the boss man, holding all the keys to our kingdom here," Brother Thomas laughed. When that was settled, the woman who'd spoken out the week before said, "It too much to work the fields, mind the babies, an' do our own cooking. We had a plantation cook where I come from."

"Well, Mary," Thomas said, bowing slightly in her direction, "you free now. So you does your own cooking."

Easter had her chance now. She stood up shyly. "Excuse me, Brother Thomas, and everybody. I . . ." She hesitated as every head turned in her direction. "I can be the nurse for the young children and make the lunch for the mothers who want me to."

"How can you do all that, daughter?" a woman asked her before Brother Thomas could answer.

Rose gazed at the sky, and Rayford glared at Easter.

"I could do it, ma'am. I know how to care for baby, and I know how to cook."

Virginia said, "It usually the old women who take care of the babies."

"And another thing," Rayford said, "how're you going to get paid?"

Brother Thomas scanned the crowd. "This girl too young for that, but there ain't no real old woman on this place."

"But I can do it," Easter protested.

Everyone talked at once. Rose, biting her lips, shook her

head in Easter's direction. Then Isabel, holding Miriam, stood up. "Excuse me, please."

Paul shushed the crowd so that his wife could speak.

"I know this girl, and she know how to handle the babies. When we run, she help me with my Miriam and she keep Miriam quiet when no one else could—not even me. I say let her do it." Isabel then turned to Easter. "You can take care of Miriam when I in the field, and I pay you twenty-five cents a week."

Easter smiled gratefully at Isabel. "Thank you," she said.

"Well, maybe it ain't a bad idea, daughter, but what about this cookin'?" Mary asked.

"I cook for the women who have the babies. Make the lunch for them while they work." Easter thought about how Mariah used to cook for the laborers in the camp.

Some of the women still looked skeptical. "Well, I don't know," one of them mused. "I use to seein' them old nurses with the babies, not no girl young as you."

"I know how to care for babies. I care for Jason since he was a baby. You could pay me whatever you want," Easter blurted out quickly.

Mary spoke again. "You can mind my Charlotte. I pay you twenty-five cents a week, like Isabel is payin' you."

Another woman stood up. "I'll let you take my two babies. I have some hens, and I been sellin' soldiers the eggs. I pay you twenty-five cents a week too. And I give you enough rice for you to fix my lunch when I workin'."

"I do the same," Mary called out.

Easter had to keep herself from grinning foolishly as the women agreed to let her take care of the children. Another woman rocked her baby. "I pay you with greens and yams from my garden and ten cent a week," she said.

Easter's eyes sparkled. She wouldn't make the two dollars that the others got, but she'd be earning some money, and she'd be out of the fields. She flashed a wide smile at Rayford.

People began to talk, and Brother Thomas hushed them.

"I hope you women is happy now. Another thing I have to say is that the missionaries suppose to be sendin' teachers to all these plantation to open school for the children."

Easter was too happy and excited to listen to any more discussions. She walked over to Rose. "You sure do know how to get what you want," Rose said as Easter approached her.

"You not angry with me, Rose?"

"No. Why should you work in the field if you ain't workin' for your own land?"

"I make Jason do his task."

"That be harder than pickin' cotton."

"Jason know if he don't work he won't get pay. I let him keep the whole two dollars. He work then."

Rayford walked over to them. "You're a clever gal, Easter. I hope you don't regret not trying to get a piece of land."

Easter spent the rest of the day cleaning an open shed near the cabins, which had been the plantation cookhouse. She was satisfied, feeling that she'd gotten something for herself.

On Monday, instead of going into the field, Easter stood outside her hut and waited for the mothers to bring the children. There were the two infants, several three- and four-year-old boys, the girls who had been chasing butter-flies, and two girls, a little older, with their baby sister.

"Good morning, Miss Easter," the girls chorused when their mother brought them to her.

She let the children play in front of the cabin while she sat on the step and watched, as she'd seen the old nurse on the Phillips plantation do. Later on in the morning she went to the shed to prepare lunch. She put the infants on the floor near her. The other children played close by, where she could watch them while she prepared a lunch of rice and cow peas. When it was time to eat lunch, Isabel and the other young mother came to nurse their infants; afterward they took the lunch out to the fields for themselves and the other women. Easter fed the rest of the children.

The infants were fast asleep, and Easter could tell that the older ones were tired. Carrying both babies, Easter took the children to a shady pine grove near the creek. They fell asleep under the trees. Easter was glad for the quiet and the chance to rest too. She spotted blades of sweet grass, almost the same kind of grass that she and Mariah had used to make their rugs and baskets. She pulled bunches of it out of the ground and found several palmetto fronds nearby. She wrapped a palmetto leaf around the grass. She'd make small rugs for all of the children to rest on, and baskets for the infants.

As she formed a pattern, one of the five-year-olds woke up. "What you doin', Miss Easter?"

"Thought you was asleep, Charlotte." Easter showed her how to make the pattern, forming at that moment the pattern of their days together.

In the evening, when Rose and the others dragged in from the fields, Easter had supper prepared. Jason plopped down onto the floor as soon as he entered the cabin. "I really goin' to get two dollars?" he asked.

Sarah rubbed her feet. "Well, least we have our own cook now."

Things were better than she'd hoped for. She got two new children when several more families came that week to live on the plantation. Since twenty-five cents seemed fair to her, she charged that amount for the new children. Even Jason was cooperating. "Anytime he slack up, I tell him he ain't gettin' his two dollars," Rose informed her.

Everything went well the following week also, until Friday. After lunch Rose stormed over to the creek. "Easter, that Jason tell me he goin' to the outhouse ten minutes ago and he not back yet."

"You watch the children. I find him for you."

Easter was angry. The other boys and girls were working, and Jason was somewhere playing. She had no idea where he was, but she walked toward the big house. Mr. Reynolds was there for inspection. A group of soldiers had come with him.

She heard laughter as she neared the house. The soldiers clapped, and one sang while another played a fife. Stepping closer to see what was happening, she spotted a little brown ankle among the long, blue-trousered legs of the soldiers.

Easter moved closer and saw Jason dancing. She pulled him by his ear, snatching him out of the circle. "Rose waitin' for you and you dancin'." He yelled as she jerked his ear again.

"Don't do that to the little tyke, girlie," one of the soldiers said, laughing. "Here's a penny for your dance, fella." A few of the other soldiers threw coins at him too.

Easter pushed Jason back to the fields. "You suppose to be workin'."

He held out his hands. "See, I made money dancing for the soldiers."

"You supposed to be makin' money in the field," she grumbled.

"You ain't in no field, Easter. Why I have to be in the field when I can get money dancing for the soldiers?"

"I take care of the children. That's my task. Dancing ain't no task." Feeling a little guilty, she let go of his arm. In a way, Jason was right. She was making him do field work, but she had managed to figure out a way of not doing it herself. "Jason, all you get is a few pennies from them soldier. Now you get two whole dollars when you work with Rose." She put her hands on his shoulders. "We leave here soon and find Obi, Jason. I promise."

"What we do after we find Obi?"

She stared at him a moment, not knowing the answer to his question. She'd only been thinking about bringing them all together.

"We find work," she said slowly, "and a place to live." She rubbed his narrow shoulders. "And no field work, Jason. The most important thing for now is we find Obi."

She kissed him impulsively on his forehead. "You go back in them fields and mind Rose."

She watched him walk slowly back to work, feeling sorry for him and for herself. *He only a child, just want to play like other children*, she thought to herself.

The women paid Easter on Saturday when they received their wages. Easter earned one dollar and sixty cents. Maybe she'd buy a dress from the cook at the big house, who sold the homespun trousers and shifts that had been made for the slaves' once-a-year clothing allotment.

On Sunday, after their church service and meeting, one of the women said to Easter, "You been a real help to me. I been able to make over two dollars this week."

Easter thanked the woman and tried not to look too proud as Rayford and Rose sat down next to her on a log. Rayford had a thin stick in his hand and began to make marks in the dirt.

"What you doin'?" Easter asked.

"Showing Rose how to write." Rayford made three marks in the dirt. "You remember what I told you this letter was, Rose?"

" 'A,' " she answered.

He then drew more marks.

She pointed, dimples decorating her face when she smiled. "That's a 'B.' "

Rayford wrote all the letters of the alphabet. "When you put these letters together you get words." He wrote the word *tree*, making the sound of each letter.

Easter was amazed. It was like magic. Those marks she'd seen on boxes and papers had names. "Do another, Rayford," she said. "Do my name."

He wrote *Easter*.

"Let me try," she said excitedly, practically snatching the stick out of his hand. She slowly tried to copy the letters of her name. "I can't make them marks like you," she said, looking at the crooked results. She handed him the stick.

He smiled slightly.

"Do Rose. How her name look?"

He wrote Rose's name.

Easter's brown, smiling eyes sparkled with excitement. "Now do Jason and then Obi and then Mariah and—"

"Easter, wait. You're too fast. You have to learn each letter first."

Rose traced over Rayford's letters with the stick. "This writin' make you happier than figurin' a way to get out of field work," she said.

"She wants to write herself a pass," Rayford commented.

"I want to write everything. M—everything that come in my head. Can I do that?"

"In time, Easter. In time."

CHAPTER
SEVEN

Before the missionary societies had dispatched their first schoolmarms to the South . . . southern blacks had taken the first step to teach themselves.

Leon F. Litwack

August 1862

By the first week in August ivory-colored petals covered the fields as the cotton flowers began to bloom. In a day the ivory petals would turn pink and start falling. Several days later the cotton bolls would burst out of their pods, and the grueling picking season would begin.

Men and women hauled the marsh mud to the field so that once all of the cotton was picked, the land would be fertilized for the winter. The rest of the hands, including the older children, worked in the vegetable garden until the cotton was ready for picking.

Easter gazed at the field while sitting at her usual shady spot by the creek. The children were having their naps. Several slept on the mats she'd made, and the infants slept in the baskets she'd coiled out of the sweet grass and palmetto fronds. When they woke, they'd help her collect more grass and palmetto leaves so that she could make additional mats.

In the meantime she was glad that they were asleep so that she could practice her letters. She picked up the stick that Julius had whittled into a sharp point at one end and scratched the letters of the alphabet in the dirt. She loved the way she could now almost form the letters as straight and pretty as Rayford did. She practiced writing her name and Rose's name and some of the words she knew: *from, house, the, is, am, tree, be, this, out, day,* and a few others.

Suddenly Jason ran over to her, his arms and legs covered with dirt. He was picking corn with the other youngsters because hauling mud was too heavy a job for them. "Easter! Easter!" he shouted.

She stood up quickly. "Not so loud. You wake the children. What happen?"

"Julius goin' to the town tomorrow to sell his corn and eggs. He say I can go with him if you say yes."

She sighed and sat down again. "You scare me. I think something terrible happen. I guess it okay. You do all your tasks?"

"Yes. Even more than I suppose to."

"You lyin' now, Jason." She smiled. "Maybe I come with you tomorrow. I never been to the town."

Easter had only left the plantation once since she'd been there. She'd accompanied Anna, Brother Thomas's wife, to the neighboring Riverview plantation. Anna went there to sell the indigo-dyed cloth she'd woven.

Jason sat down next to her, putting his arms around her neck. "Maybe we see Obi there."

Easter rested her stick on the ground. "Yes, Jason. He may be right in the town thinkin' about us."

"I have to tell Julius I goin' with him tomorrow." Jason stood up and headed toward the small wooden bridge that would take him to the other side of the creek, where the field hands were shoveling the marsh mud onto oxcarts.

As the day wore on, Easter wove daydreams about finding Obi in town. The best part of the daydreams was when he held her around her waist and kissed her like he had when he left the Confederate camp.

That evening, while she cooked their usual dinner of

cow peas and rice, she told the others about her trip to town. "Me and Jason goin' with Julius."

Melissa looked at her as if she were crazy. "Tomorrow Saturday. We suppose to be workin' on the quilt," she reminded Easter.

"Remember you say you help me in the field tomorrow?" Rose called from outside of the hut as she cleaned off her muddy arms and legs. "I have two more cart of mud to fill, then I finish my task."

Easter had forgotten that yesterday she'd promised to help Rose when Rose had come in tired and complaining that she could not finish her work without some help. "What about Rayford?" Easter asked. "He can't help you?"

"Rayford have he own fields to work."

"But I finish all my tasks, so I can go," Jason squeaked from the corner.

Easter narrowed her eyes at him. "I have to stay and do chores, and you have chores too," she said.

"But you promise me, Easter. You bein' evil 'cause you can't go," he shouted, tears trickling down his cheeks.

Easter wanted to cry also. Instead she shouted back, "That's right. I have to do chores and so do you. Keep sassin' me and I give you a spanking."

"That old town ain't movin' nowhere," Sarah said. "You go some other time."

"Seem like Julius ought to have something to do besides go to the town," Rose added as she entered the room. She stared at Jason. "What you cryin' like a baby for? Easter be right. You have chores to do."

Jason stood up quickly and dashed outside as Rayford entered the room. "What's wrong with him?" Rayford asked.

Easter uncovered the three-legged iron pot in which the rice was cooking. "Food ready now," she said. "Y'all eat. I goin' to find Jason."

Rayford stopped her. "Wait, Easter. I have some good

news. The missionaries are sending a teacher. We're going to have a school right on this plantation."

"That's wonderful," Melissa said, her broad face breaking out into a large smile. "These children learn how to read and write."

Rayford sat down on the bench. "Adults too. There'll be a night class for adults."

"Where they goin' to have class?" Sarah asked. "In the cotton field?"

"We're going to build a schoolhouse and church in one. Mr. Reynolds said we can cut down some of those trees near the end of the fields for lumber."

Easter's heavy mood lightened at the thought of going to school. "Guess I learn how to read and write fast now," she said.

"Yes," Rayford said. "I hope the missionaries send books with the teachers." Rayford had been bringing in old newspapers when he found them, so that Easter could practice her reading.

"Let me tell Jason," she said. She left the hut. But as she searched for Jason, she softened, and in the end she decided to let him go to town with Julius.

Easter and Rose were ankle deep in marsh mud on the other side of the creek. Easter's loathing of field work reached new depths as she threw a shovelful of mud into the oxcart, breathing in the scent of what seemed to be rotten eggs each time they lifted the mud. Rose stopped for a moment, staring at Easter's unhappy face as if she were reading her thoughts. "Least we gettin' pay," she said.

"Rose, they ain't payin' us enough for this work."

"Well, at least we getting' our own land, then."

"You sound like a Rayford echo," Easter answered sarcastically.

They finished by the afternoon. Easter bathed in the tin tub and put on her one other dress, a blue and white checked gingham purchased from the cook. "One dollar too much to pay for that old dress. It ain't new," Rose had said. "The cook settin' up there in the big house gettin' rich, sellin' everything the Yankee didn't take." After Easter removed the dirty scarf from around her head and braided her thick black hair, she felt better.

The women brought the bench out of the hut and put it under a shady tree near the cabin. They sat there working steadily on the quilt. Easter felt a kind of peacefulness come over her spirit as she listened to their talk. Rose related the week's news, and Easter smiled slightly to herself, wondering how Rose could get so much information about folks' business when she was in a cotton field all day.

Easter's mind began to drift away from their talk. Once the winter came, she'd find a little more time to move around. Next Saturday she'd go to the town. She'd make sure not to promise to help with anything. She and Jason would go and look around for Obi. She'd also find out where every plantation on the island was located, and she'd visit them all in search of Obi.

They worked on the quilt until the sun started to slide behind the tops of the trees and the sound of the men's chopping stopped. "Guess Jason and Julius be along soon," she said as she and Melissa dragged the bench back inside the cabin.

They all helped to prepare supper, and Easter expected Jason to come bursting through the door any minute with a lot of talk and excitement. It was Rayford, though, who walked in. "Jason and Julius not back yet?" he asked. "Julius probably walked in the wrong direction. This is an island, so they can't get lost," he said reassuringly.

Jason and Julius hadn't returned when the food was ready. "We eat now and save Jason his meal," Easter said.

Easter took her plate and sat cross-legged on Mariah's mat. "I hope Jason behave. Hope he an' Julius ain't get separated."

Rayford took a long swallow of water. "Don't worry. The

town isn't that big," he said. "Brother Thomas took me there last week."

Easter detected that even though Rayford tried to sound calm, he was somewhat worried. When another hour passed and Jason and Julius still hadn't returned, Rayford walked to the door. "I'm getting Brother Thomas, and we're going to look for them."

"I want to go too, Rayford," Easter said.

"No. You stay here. We'll find them."

Rayford left; in a few minutes he returned with Brother Thomas, George, Paul, and some of the other men, all carrying their shotguns and rifles. Brother Thomas's heavy frame seemed to fill up the hut. "I wish I know they was goin' to the town. I send my son, James, with them. They should never stay there after dark. These woods be dangerous. When the rich rice planters leave, them poor whites take to hidin' in the woods from the Yankee. White and colored people have some mighty wars goin' on amongst them trees and—"

"Brother," Rayford said, cutting off Thomas's speech, "think we better get going."

Rose put her arm around Easter's shoulders. "They'll find them."

Easter wasn't so sure. She wanted to run outside and look for Jason herself. *Why did I let him go?* she asked herself over and over.

The men were about to leave the hut when suddenly one shouted, "Someone's comin'!"

Jason came dashing into the cabin, and Julius rushed in breathlessly behind him. They all crowded around them, everyone asking questions at once. Easter was so relieved that she collapsed weakly onto the rug, letting the tension leave her body.

Julius sat on the bench and wiped his high forehead with a handkerchief. "Let me catch a breath," he said.

While Julius calmed himself, Jason rattled out the story. "We had a time. The town is the biggest thing I ever see.

Julius sell all he corn and egg, and I make three dollar dancin' for the Yankee soldiers." He held out a fistful of change to show them all. "Then when we was comin' back, the hants chase us."

Rayford looked disgusted. "Boy, there ain't no such thing as hants and ghosts."

The other men laughed. "That weren't no ghosts you saw," Brother Thomas said. "It was them whites livin' in the woods."

"That's what I try to tell him," Julius said, still gasping for breath. "Everything was fine until we head home. We in the woods way 'cross from the other side of the creek when these white men come from nowhere."

"That's right," Jason said. "They fly out the trees."

"Jason, hush your foolishness," Julius said. "The men try, but they can't catch us. We out run them."

Brother Thomas took the floor. "Listen, y'all. First, you don't know this island like we people who been livin' here do. Second, them woods be dangerous. Even the road be dangerous. Them buckra like to catch some unsuspecting one of us. Colored people even been rob and killed." His voice started to rise as if he were preaching. "There be runaway Rebel soldier in them woods, and I reckon even some runaway Yankee. No one better leave this plantation," he warned gravely. "We almost lose Jason and Julius. Nobody go farther than the Riverview plantation."

Easter's heart sank. How would she ever find Obi if she couldn't go any farther than the Riverview plantation? Maybe Brother Thomas was just making things sound worse than they really were.

"Excuse me Brother Thomas," she said. "But is things really dangerous like you say?"

"Daughter, I warning you. Better take heed." He paused and stared at Jason. "You too young man take heed. A lot of these buckra want to see us colored people dead. They blaming this war on us. If you roam about this place you 'bout as safe as a lamb in a lion's den."

CHAPTER
EIGHT

*The whole world opened to me when I learned to read. As
soon as I understood something, I rushed back and taught it
to the others at home.*

Mary McLeod Bethune

May 1863

" 'Rem . . . re . . . re—' I mean, 'Remem—mem—' Oh,
Miss Grantley, I can't read this," Easter said.

Miss Grantley was the young white teacher sent to the
plantation by the Northern Missionary Society. On Sundays the teacher's pine table became an altar for either
Brother Thomas or a visiting preacher.

"Come now, Easter," Miss Grantley said. "Try again.
The word is 'remember.' "

Easter sighed loudly and clutched the Bible tightly as she
stood in front of the combination classroom and church
that the men on the plantation had built.

" 'Remem—remember this day in which ye came out
from . . .' " She stared blankly at the teacher.

"Egypt," Miss Grantley said. "Now try to read it without
stumbling. Take your time."

" 'Remember this day in which ye came out from E . . .
E . . . Egypt, out of the house of bond . . . bondage.' "

"You have to practice the words you stumbled over
Easter, but that was somewhat better."

"Yes ma'am," Easter said, and handed the Bible to Nathan, who stood next to her. She resumed her seat on the bench as Nathan stumbled and lurched over the rest of the passage: " 'For by stren . . .' "

"Strength," Miss Grantley said patiently as she glanced out of the corner of her eye at the restless younger children on the other side of the room.

" 'For by strength of hand,' " David continued, " 'the Lord brung—' "

"Brought."

" 'Brought you out from this here—' "

"Nathan, I don't think you see the word 'here.' "

"No, ma'am, I mean to say, 'the Lord brought you out from this place.' " He handed Miss Grantley the Bible and sat next to Easter.

The students sat on benches on either side of the room. There was a fireplace and one window in the back. Since new refugees continued to arrive on the plantation, the makeshift schoolroom was full. Every child had his or her own slate and chalk. While Easter attended class, she still had the care of two new babies and the infants, who were now a year old.

At about fifteen years of age, Easter was the oldest student in the class. The two baskets containing the new babies were next to her on the bench. Jason, who was nine years old, sat at the opposite end of the room with the younger children. There were no pens, ink, or paper, and only a Bible and a few geography books for the older students. But there was a long piece of slate on the wall installed by the men when they built the one-room log house. Easter lived for the time she spent in school. She no longer had trouble understanding the funny Yankee talk, but she had to remember to try to arrange words Miss Grantley's way when she was talking to her.

Miss Grantley pushed her glasses up on her nose and addressed the older students. "Practice your reading while I see to the rest of the students. And Easter, when you've completed your reading, help the little ones with their penmanship." The teacher wrote spelling words on the blackboard for Jason and the other students in the middle group. Miriam and another year-old child played around everyone's feet.

Easter picked up her geography and for a while was transported to places that only a few months ago she never knew existed. When she finished her assignment, she helped the younger children. As usual, the morning sped, and it seemed no time at all before Miss Grantley's voice rang out, "School's over, children."

Jason and the other boys were the first ones out of the room. "Go straight to Rose," Easter called after him. All of the children over six worked in the fields in the afternoon after their morning classes. Miss Grantley would leave to teach at a nearby plantation. She'd then come back to the Williams plantation to conduct an evening class for the adults.

Easter gathered up the sleeping infants and called Miriam and the other child.

"Easter, before you leave I want to talk with you," Miss Grantley said as she piled the children's slates neatly on her table.

"Yes ma'am?" Easter's hair, grown back to its original length, was braided and coiled in a bun. She wore her neat blue and white gingham dress and was as graceful and willowy as the blades of grass she used for her baskets.

Miss Grantley adjusted her little round glasses, which seemed always to slide down her thin nose. "Easter, you are learning everything so quickly. If you continued your studies, you could be a wonderful student."

"Thank you, ma'am," Easter said proudly. She liked Miss Grantley and often wondered whether all Yankee women were as kind as she was.

"The missionary society has a school in Philadelphia for superior colored students. I'm going to ask them to sponsor you. I could try and get them to cover some of your costs—

and maybe we could find a good colored family for you to live with." She pushed a wisp of her wavy brown hair out of her eyes. "You would be the first student freed from slavery that the school ever had. Easter, would you like to go north, to Philadelphia?"

Easter's mind flashed to the missionary lady who'd offered to carry her and Jason north. She smiled as she remembered how frightened she was of the woman. Then she remembered why she hadn't wanted to leave at that time.

"I can't leave here. I have to find Obi," she said.

"Who is Obi?" Miss Grantley asked. She listened intently as Easter related her history. "You can come back and seek him out when you complete school," Miss Grantley said when Easter had finished.

"I love school, but I can't leave. What about Jason? Can't leave him."

Miss Grantley pressed her thin lips together and shook her head. "Jason wouldn't do too well at the school. He's smart, but he doesn't care about school—or anything serious, I'm afraid—the way you do."

Easter knew that Miss Grantley was right about Jason, but that made no difference to her. "I can't leave Jason. And then, I so far away from Obi."

"Easter, you don't know exactly where Obi is. And Jason, well, he can stay here with Rose."

"Oh no, Miss Grantley. Jason has to come with me."

"Well, maybe he can come with you and go to school in a colored orphanage. But I hate to see someone like you not get the education that she deserves." She looked worried as she rested her hand on Easter's shoulder. "And you know, Easter, when you finish your studies, you can come back here and teach your own people. There's much work to be done."

Easter faltered. "Miss Grantley, I don't know, I . . ."

"Will you think about it? You'd be a wonderful teacher.

You can return when the war ends and find your young man then."

"Suppose it never ends."

"Wars always end, sometime."

"Suppose Yankee don't win, and I up north. I never get back here."

Easter could tell that Miss Grantley seemed a little concerned. She tried to put a confident smile on her face. "We're going to win. It's just a matter of time."

Easter left the school feeling herself pulled two different ways. She gripped the two baskets tightly as she passed the cabins and headed toward the cookhouse. It would be wonderful to go to school and learn how to read *all* of the books. She'd be like Miss Grantley, a good, fine teacher. But how could she leave Jason? What would happen to him without her?

And what about Obi? Suppose he was nearby this minute, searching for her? He'd never find her up north. She even thought about Mariah and Gabriel. If she went north, she'd probably never see them again.

Charlotte pulled at her skirt. "Miss Easter, you tellin' us a story? Then you an' me make baskets?"

"Yes, baby."

"Me too?" Charlotte's younger sister asked.

"Yes." Easter smiled at her and checked the field to see whether Jason was there. She spotted him by the Yankee cap that one of the soldiers who sometimes came to the plantation had given him.

Easter placed the babies' baskets on the ground when she reached the shed. Her mind wandered as she began to fix lunch. For some reason everything she saw seemed beautiful: the blue sky and the orchards; the southern pines and palmettoes and live oak trees with the moss hanging from their branches like cobwebs; the green fields and pastures. What was the North like? She'd mostly heard that it was cold.

That evening while they ate, she watched the faces of

her friends, and they seemed beautiful too. Her heart felt heavy when she looked at them and thought about going north. She might never see them again either.

They sat at a pine table that Paul had made for them. He'd also made another bench so that they all could eat at the table. Easter's rugs and several baskets decorated the wall. The hut was overcrowded but cozy, made livable by the women.

As she watched Rayford eat, she thought she'd miss even him. Although he was bossy, Easter had to agree with Rose, who said, "What Rayford say is most times correct, Easter." She'd always be thankful to him for being the first person to teach her how to read and write. He'd smile pleasantly at her when he walked by as she was caring for the babies, even though he'd still say, "You need to get some land."

They usually ate in silence. "Too hungry to talk," Rose would comment. But this evening it seemed that all Rose and Rayford did was talk, which was unlike Rayford. Easter wanted to ask them what they thought about her going north, but she couldn't get a chance to say anything. Even Melissa noticed Rayford's changed personality.

"You actin' like a young boy, old man," she joked.

"He ain't no old man," Rose defended him. Her dark eyes seemed livelier than usual. Then she hesitated as if she had something else to say but wasn't certain how to say it. "We been livin' like a family, so I guess you'll be the first to get the news—me and Rayford is marryin'. A real marriage too. No slave marriage, where someone could sell him away from me or me away from him."

"That's why I never married before," Rayford added, "because it didn't mean anything." He rubbed Rose's arm. "And I never met anyone as beautiful as Rose."

"Or who could cook like Rose." Sarah winked.

Easter found her voice. She knew there was a special feeling between Rose and Rayford, but marriage? She never thought of that. "Oh, Rose, it's wonderful," she said, embracing her.

Rose frowned. "We have to find a minister who will marry us."

Easter waved her hand. "You could find a minister easy."

Rayford picked up his spoon. "One preacher already refused. Said that just because President Lincoln signed that Emancipation Proclamation doesn't mean we're really free. He said maybe we weren't slaves, but we weren't citizens either."

"And another preacher refused too," Rose added. "He say we belong to the Yankee now, so let them marry us."

"Pull up them long faces," Melissa said. "You'll find a preacher, and we goin' to have a celebration." As Rose, Melissa, and Sarah chatted about the wedding, Easter decided not to say anything about her problem. She'd have to make her own decision in the end, so she joined their conversation.

"And that ain't all, Easter," Rose said excitedly. "Mr. Reynolds say we can buy one of them cottages near the big house that used to be for the house servants on this place. We have two whole rooms."

Easter tried to concentrate on Rose's conversation but she couldn't help thinking about Obi. Wondering whether they'd ever be together again. And a thought she'd never had before—whether someday they'd be like Rose and Rayford and get married. But suppose she went north? What would happen then?

"Easter!" Rose said. "You ain't listening to a word I saying."

"Yes, I am, Rosie. I thinking about marriages and weddings. And we have to get busy to make you a good wedding."

Easter and the other women prepared for the wedding, even though no one knew when it would take place. "We'll be ready when it happen," Isabel said as she wove the cotton yarn in the spinning house one evening for Rose's wedding dress.

Easter picked up the carding brush so that she could comb the cotton fibers. "Maybe they could get that preacher who visit here sometime," she suggested.

"He boring," Isabel said.

Another woman who was helping them laughed. "It only take ten minutes to say them marriage words. We tell him to just marry Rose and Rayford and don't preach."

The wedding preparations helped Easter forget her own problems for a while. Rayford shook his head one evening as he watched Easter hem the white cotton dress Isabel had made for Rose. "You know what look right pretty, Rose?" Easter asked. "Isabel get some more of this cloth and we wrap your head in it."

"Oh no. That look like I workin' in the field," Rose protested.

Easter thought about Mariah. "The old grandmother down at the coast tell me that in Africa only the important women tie their head in white cloth."

Rayford smiled at them. "You womenfolk gone mad on this plantation. We still don't have a preacher to marry us. I found out that the visiting white preacher's not licensed to marry or bury anybody. He's like our Brother Thomas."

Rose fingered the dress. "We find somebody."

"In the meantime," Melissa said, "we ain't had nothing to celebrate in years. Now we do."

Rayford came home with the good news a week later. He'd found a judge who'd marry them. "We have two names now," he told Rose. "We have to sign a paper before a judge, and the judge will marry us tomorrow. It'll be legal."

Easter grinned happily. "Now we have our wedding."

Melissa put the wooden plates on the table. "Tomorrow is Sunday. A fine day for a marriage."

"I glad I learn how to write some. I can sign my own name. What's my second name, Rayford?"

"I picked my father's first name. I remember my mother

told me that their master called him Sam, but his real name was Sabay. So I am now Rayford Sabay." He held out his hand and bowed to Rose. "And this is my wife, Rose Sabay."

Easter liked the sound of Rose's new name. If she ever had to get a second name, she had no idea what it would be. She thought about Obi. *Easter Obi*, she thought, giggling to herself, *that sounds right silly*.

CHAPTER
NINE

My mother's sons were angry with me,
*   they made me keeper of the vineyards;*
*   but, my own vineyard I have not kept!*

Song of Solomon 1:6

June 1863
God smilin' on us today, Easter thought. Everyone was there, even the cook, who only associated with them when she had something to sell. The sky was clear and blue and the air smelled of pine, and the pink and white magnolia trees were still in bloom.

It was a day far removed from the blood and pain and horror of war and bondage. Instead of having church service inside the log house, they decided the Sunday service should be held outside, "under God's roof," as Brother Thomas said. Service would begin when Rose and Rayford returned from the judge who would marry them.

Everyone had brought a bench, a box, or a chair to sit on. Tables covered with oilcloth were placed near the kitchen shed. People brought whatever food they could spare, and Easter and some of the other women had stayed up late into the night baking pies.

Julius sat in front of Easter. Every minute he turned around to say something to her. "Will you write to me when I join the army?"

"Yes. I told you I would. But when you get to them other islands, remember to ask about Obi."

"Okay," he said, looking disappointed. "But when I get to the other island, mostly I remember how pretty you look today."

Easter wore a new homespun dress that Isabel had made for her. Isabel had dyed it with indigo, and the violet shade complemented Easter's nut brown complexion. She'd let out her black hair, which framed her face like a dark, cottony mist. Miss Grantley sat next to her, and Easter hoped that she wouldn't ask her about going north today. She didn't want to think about anything that might trouble her.

The crowd stirred; they'd spotted Rose and Rayford walking toward them. James, Brother Thomas's son, had driven them to the judge in his wagon. Everyone clapped and stood up when the couple neared them. Rayford waved the marriage license like a flag. Rose's unblemished mahogany-colored skin was enhanced by the white dress and head wrap. Rayford wore the white pants and shirt that he used to wear on the Phillips plantation.

"They are a handsome couple," Miss Grantley murmured, adjusting her glasses.

Brother Thomas sat them in front of everyone else. Julius turned around to Easter. "Bet you look as beautiful as Rose when you get marry."

"Hush," was all she said as her face grew warm. She hoped that Julius wouldn't pester her all day long.

They had all scrubbed themselves and had mended and washed their garments and made as fine an appearance as they could muster for Rayford and Rose. Jason wore his Sunday pants, a pair of long trousers that must have belonged to one of the former master's children. Easter was angry at him for paying the cook two dollars for the trousers and another ruffled shirt. She snatched his Yankee forage cap off his head. "We havin' church," she whispered. There were gingham dresses and homespun dresses dyed various shades of blue, overalls, trousers, and plaid shirts, and in some cases, suits. Brother Thomas's smile was as broad as his back as he stepped before the congregation.

"We have a marriage to celebrate," Virginia shouted. "Don't preach into Eternity, Brother Thomas."

Easter thanked God for the day and then blocked out Thomas's oratory, thinking about Obi instead—imagining that she and Obi were sitting where Rose and Rayford were. She then joined in the singing, which was particularly joyful that Sunday. When the church service was over, several women brought out sweet potato pies and placed them on one of the tables. Samuel, Elias, and some of the other men had dug a barbecue pit.

Julius nudged Easter. "The only part of that pig they ain't cookin' is the oink."

"I have to go and help the women bring the food out," she said, and left her seat to go to the cooking shed. She wanted to get away from Julius.

Easter helped bring out the steaming bowls of rice and peas. Some of the men had gone hunting for wild turkey, against army regulations. Easter glanced at Rose, who blossomed as she sat like a queen greeting her friends. Rayford stood behind her, his hands on her shoulders. He smiled happily. *Never knew Rayford was so handsome,* Easter said to herself as she returned to the cooking shed.

"I never see Mister Ray smile like he doin' today," Isabel remarked as she helped Easter pile more rice into a bowl.

"Hope he don't hurt he face," Easter joked. She looked at Sarah, who stood next to her, carving the turkey. "What's wrong?" she asked, and was shocked when tears streamed down Sarah's weary face.

"I had a husband one time, but it was only a slave marriage. He was sold away. I never see him again."

Melissa stopped what she was doing and put her arms around Sarah. "Don't think about that. Things changin' now, can't you see?"

Easter watched the two women. *There's always something*

sad to think about, even during a happy time, she said to herself. She scanned the people milling around the tables, but she didn't see Jason. "Jason suppose to be helpin' us carry this food out," she said to Virginia.

"There he is with the banjo picker." Virginia pointed beyond the tables.

"We can forget about help from him once Weston start pluckin' that banjo," Mary remarked. People started clapping to the banjo's rhythm, and Jason moved his lithe body as if he were being plucked like one of the strings. Even Miss Grantley clapped as she watched Jason.

"Folks are enjoyin' Jason so much they'll get mad if I make him come and help us," Easter said, bobbing her head to the music.

After everyone had eaten, the celebration really began. Brother Thomas's voice was heard everywhere. He shouted to one of his sons, "James, get that wagon and go fetch the old fiddler from the Johnson place!"

Brother Thomas's wife, Anna, who'd always lived on the plantation, snapped her fingers. "That old man make these trees dance," she said.

James returned with an old man who could hardly climb out of the wagon. Easter tried not to laugh when Mary said, "He look like he can't even hold the fiddle, much less play it."

He toddled over to Weston, slowly adjusting his instrument under his chin. But when he fiddled, it was as if he had magic in his bow. No foot was still. He and Weston played, and Rayford and Rose led the circle of dancers. Melissa took Elias's hand and they too joined the dancers.

Julius approached Easter with his hand out and a grin on his face. She accepted his hand and was caught in the old fiddler's magic, forgetting for a while about Obi, Miss Grantley, and going north.

The next day was work as usual for everyone. Rose was back in her fields, with a worn-out Jason helping her in the

afternoon. Easter knew that she'd have to give Miss Grantley an answer soon, and as she walked from her hut to the
school, she made her decision.

Even Miss Grantley tried to stifle several yawns as she
pried answers out of her weary students. When the class
was over, Easter approached her.

"Miss Grantley, I can't leave Jason here, and I can't leave
without knowing where Obi is." She averted her eyes from
the teacher's disappointed face. "Suppose Obi come here
and no one know where I am?"

"We can leave word, Easter. Rayford or Rose or any one
of the people here could tell him where you are."

"Suppose Rose and Rayford leave, and these other people
forget where you tell them I gone 'cause you leave too.
People comin' and goin' all the time."

Miss Grantley sighed. "That they are, Easter. But I don't
think your going north will hurt your chances of finding
Obi."

"Another thing too, ma'am. I don't know nothing about
the North."

"Easter, I'll write to the commander on Hilton Head
Island where I hear colored soldiers are being trained. You
say Obi is just a little older than you, so there's a good
chance that he is a soldier."

"Oh no, Miss Grantley. Soldiers get killed." Easter tried
to control herself, but she couldn't stop the tears. "Maybe
he dead."

"Easter, don't think such thoughts. I'm sure he's as alive
as you and I."

Easter wiped her face. How, she wondered, could Miss
Grantley be so sure of that.

"If we find him and you are able to bring Jason with you,
would you agree to go then?"

"Yes, I think so. But I have to find him."

Miss Grantley took off her glasses. Her green eyes
searched Easter's face. "I sense something else keeping you

here. In order to move forward, sometimes we have to sever ties. You have your own life, Easter."

"I don't understand, ma'am."

"I mean . . . well, someday Jason will go his own way. And Obi too."

"Oh no. Obi is going to look for me. I know it." The conversation was taking the shape of the conversations she'd had with Rose and Rayford. Her feelings were in her heart, and words could not express what was there.

"Easter, your life belongs to you now."

"But what is my life if I not with Jason and Obi, and in the North who is there to tell me, 'Easter, you better not do that because it's dangerous?' Or, 'Easter, you better work the fields or you won't get land.' " She smiled as she imitated Rayford's deep voice. "Or, 'Easter, we like sisters.' "

"I understand—I think. But we have to let go of certain things in order to move forward," Miss Grantley said again.

"How can you let go the only people you have?"

Miss Grantley had no answer. "I'll write the letter to the army commander's office and find out what we can about your young man," she said.

By the end of the year an answer to Miss Grantley's letter arrived. One afternoon after class Miss Grantley showed Easter the letter. "The army is very slow. There were men from the mainland and from many of the islands sent to Hilton Head Island for training in January. The army has no idea where they went or even what their names were. Many of them took new names once they joined." She adjusted her glasses. "We'll keep trying, Easter."

Easter left class that day feeling helpless and wondering whether she should forget about trying to find Obi. But she couldn't forget him; the disappointing letter from the army only seemed to make her think about him more. Julius and a few other young men left the plantation and joined the Union army. Once again, Easter promised to write Julius and reminded him to make inquiries about Obi.

The beginning of 1864 brought more changes. One day, after school had ended, Easter was in the cookinghouse preparing lunch. Miss Grantley, looking flushed and upset, rushed into the shed.

"What happen?" Easter asked, afraid of the answer.

The teacher bit her lip. "I just received this letter," she said, her voice cracking slightly. Easter thought it was another letter from the army in answer to the additional inquiries Miss Grantley had made about Obi. "I'm being sent by the society to open a school on another island. I'll be leaving here shortly."

"Oh no, Miss Grantley. You're *our* teacher. Nobody else can be a teacher for us."

Miss Grantley removed her glasses and brushed her hands over her eyes. "The society is sending another teacher."

"Why can't the new teacher open the school and you stay here with us?"

"I . . . I have more experience with starting a school."

Easter picked up one of the babies, who'd begun to whimper. "It won't be the same with another teacher," she said. "It won't feel right, Miss Grantley." Easter tried to push back the tears welling up in her eyes. "When they sending this new teacher?"

"I don't know. There don't seem to be enough teachers to go around."

"This is terrible. There'll be no school at all, and we'll miss you."

Miss Grantley put on her glasses and cleared her throat. "I begged the society to let me stay for at least another year, but I was told that I must leave. I'll miss all of you, especially you, Easter." She placed her hand on Easter's shoulder. "I'll write you."

"Me too. I'll write every day."

"And Easter, you run the school until the new teacher comes. You can do it."

"I can't. I don't know too much my ownself."

"You can. You know how to teach those little ones their letters and numbers."

"But what about the geography and the arithmetic and the history and . . ."

Miss Grantley smiled slightly. "Just teach what you know, and that's plenty. One day you'll come to the school in Philadelphia. Promise, Easter." Before Easter could say anything, however, Miss Grantley said, "No. That's not fair, to make you promise such a thing now. Think about coming to the school. Will you promise to do that?" The teacher took off her glasses and wiped her eyes again.

Easter nodded, having to force back tears herself. "I promise," she barely whispered.

CHAPTER
TEN

My army cross over,
My army cross over,
O, Pharoah's army drownded!
My army cross over

Traditional Spiritual

May 1865

Easter walked quickly past the former slave market in town, imagining a long white arm pulling her inside its dark corners. The sidewalk was choked with people: men and women, whites and blacks, destitute families, prosperous-looking men who seemed not to have been touched by war at all, and Union soldiers.

Easter enjoyed looking in the window of a dress shop that always had a lovely dark blue satin dress with burgundy ruffles down the front and a wide-brimmed burgundy hat to match. The shop had been closed since she'd been coming to Elenaville. As she walked away, she wondered whether she'd ever own such a fine dress.

Jason skipped ahead of her in wide-eyed excitement. There was a chorus of peddlars. A woman passed them carrying a large basket of eggs on her head. She sang the praises of her produce:

Fresh eggs brown and white,
Yellow and sweet inside.

A man pulling a wagonload of catfish, shrimp, and other seafood sang his song also, on the opposite side of the street:

I have shrimp and catfish,
Oyster and clam.
Buy from me,
Your fish-sellin' man.

This was the third time since the war ended in April that she, Sarah, and some of the other people from the plantation had come to the Freedmen's Bureau office in Elenaville to inquire about relatives. Easter came seeking information about Obi. Brother Thomas still warned them, "Don't walk—especially through them woods—an' get back here before dark." James drove them. Passengers riding in the wagon paid him ten cents to carry them back and forth. Once the war was over and people from the plantation started traveling to town more often, Jason constantly begged her to take him to Elenaville. She couldn't come without him.

Easter hurried to catch up with the others. The office of the Freedmen's Bureau was packed with people, outside and in. There were whites sprinkled among the blacks.

"Can I stay outside?" Jason asked when Easter was able to enter the building after waiting for two hours on one of the lines outside.

"Yes, but you stay right here on this street. Don't go runnin' off with no little vagabonds."

"Listen to Easter and stay close by," Sarah added.

"I will! I will!" he shouted excitedly.

People sat and stood in every corner of the large room, which had once been used as a warehouse for storing cotton. A few bales were still stacked along a wall. A woman and two men sat behind separate desks. They took care of supplying people with emergency rations of food and money, helping people find lost family members, and even starting schools. They also made sure that the work contracts that were being used to hire the freedmen and freedwomen to work on the plantations were in order.

Easter sat on the floor with Sarah and the rest of the people and waited, hoping that this time someone would be able to tell her where Obi was. Time seemed to stop in the crowded room, and when her turn came to talk to one of the agents, she had a pounding headache.

"Afternoon, ma'am," she said politely as she sat down. The woman's brown wavy hair reminded her of Miss Grantley. Easter repeated her scanty information about Obi once again. Her headache eased as she talked. The woman thumbed through a thick record book.

"Oh yes, you were here two weeks ago. I'm sorry, we have no record of anyone by that name."

Easter sighed deeply.

"I'm very sorry," the woman repeated. "You said he escaped here to the Sea Islands. We wrote to the Freedmen's Bureau in Georgetown, but there's no response from them yet. We're attempting to make inquiries with the army, but they have so much to do, don't you know."

And they slow as a snail, don't you know, Easter said to herself. Easter tried to contain the horrible thought that Obi had been killed in battle and left dead somewhere. "Ma'am, does the army know all the soldiers that die, even colored soldiers?"

"Of course. Unfortunately, sometimes soldiers are missing, but the army keeps track of everyone as best they can. You say your former master's name is Jennings? Your friend may have taken that name. We'll make another inquiry and find out whether they have a soldier named Obi Jennings."

"Thank you, ma'am," Easter said dully. When she left the building, the sun was red and sinking. She immediately scanned the crowd, but she didn't see Jason.

James's wagon was parked in front of the Protestant Episcopal Church on the town square. She ran over to the wagon. Everyone except Jason was there. "Where Jason?" she almost shrieked.

James pointed to a group of people surrounding a tall white man who stood in front of a brightly painted carriage. Easter read the fancy orange and black lettering on its front: DR. TAYLOR'S TONIC. The man's thick brown mustache covered his upper lip. He held up a bottle. Another white man stood next to him, dressed in a bright yellow shirt and red pantaloons, with a red scarf around his forehead. He held a fiddle. Easter had never seen anyone dressed in such an outlandish fashion. A big gold-colored hoop earring dangled from his ear, and his black mustache looked like a crow's wings.

The man with the bottle addressed the crowd. "Doctor yourself with Dr. Taylor's formula, and you'll never need a doctor again. This ain't no snake oil," he assured them. "Now for a bit of entertainment from our little dancing Indian."

The man in the red pantaloons squatted before a tom-tom and beat out a rhythm. A lithe brown figure wearing an Indian headdress that was too big charged out of the carriage. The figure jumped up and down, whooping and hollering. Then the man picked up his fiddle, and the Indian did a familiar dance. The crowd cheered.

Easter tried to reach the carriage, but there were too many people blocking her way. When the dance ended, everyone rushed closer to the carriage to buy the tonic, and Easter was swept along with the crowd.

"Jason! You fool little jack-a-behind. Get off that carriage!" she yelled.

The man with the brown mustache jumped off the little stage jutting out of the carriage and let the man in the red pantaloons sell the medicine. "Girlie," he said clamping his hands on Easter's shoulders, "this little lad is bringing me luck. Are you his sister?"

Jason grinned at her guiltily. "I he sister, he mother, and he father. And he better get over here to me." She glared at Jason.

"Girlie, I'll pay the lad well and take good care of him. Let him join my show."

Jason jumped off the carriage and stood next to her. "Easter, let me be in the show."

"No!"

"Where do ye live, lad?" the man asked before Easter could pull Jason away.

"The Williams plantation," Jason called to the man.

Easter pulled him through the crowd toward the wagon. "I thought I lose you, Jason."

"Easter," he said, stretching out his hand, "I made one whole dollar and didn't have to be in no fields. Can I stay in the man's show? Please, Easter?"

"No. You don't know what kind of evil man he could be. And that other mad-looking man, who he suppose to be?"

"That's Percy the Pirate. Please, let me stay."

James laughed as Easter and Jason reached the wagon. "That man sold plenty snake oil this day."

Jason's brown eyes pleaded with Easter. "I'll come back to visit you, Easter, and I write you and—"

"You can't be in nothing like that. How you know that man really take care of you?" Easter asked as she and Jason climbed up onto the wagon seat.

"Easter's right," James remarked as he patted the two mules. "Men like that goes from place to place like boll weevils. Sometime they don't make no money at all." He climbed up beside them.

"But you see different places, and you make money an' you have fun." Jason's face shone with excitement as he stared longingly at the medicine man's carriage.

James lifted the reins, and the mules moved slowly out of the square.

It was dusk when they headed into the countryside, and when they neared the plantation it was dark. Easter gazed at the sky. The night was clear and the stars large and bright. "Jason," she whispered, "the angels smilin' at us."

He ignored her and rattled on about Dr. Taylor's medicine show. She kept staring at the sky as she listened to the sound of his voice.

Easter felt their lives changing. A new season was upon them. When the missionaries sent another teacher, she and Jason would leave the plantation. She made up her mind not to return to the Freedmen's Bureau. She had saved most of the money she had earned over the last three years; she would use that money to travel to the other islands and look for Obi herself. She would also go to the old Confederate camp and look up Mariah and Gabriel. After she found Obi, she and Jason would go north so that she could finish her schooling. Then she would come back to South Carolina, and she and Obi and Jason would be together forever.

CHAPTER
ELEVEN

May 29, 1865, President Johnson issues a proclamation giving a general amnesty . . . to those who have participated in the rebellion against Federal authority . . . all property rights except those in slaves will be fully restored.

From *The Civil War Almanac*

The next evening, Easter sat with Rose and Rayford in their large and comfortable kitchen. The wooden dishes were lined neatly along the mantel, and several skillets of various sizes hung above it. An iron stove stood near the pantry, and the large rug Easter had made for their wedding present was spread under the cane-seat rocker. One of Easter's students had made Rose's sewing basket, which lay on the floor beside the rocking chair. A set of keys hung near the door. Since Rayford was the overseer, he had all of the keys to the outbuildings. Mr. Reynolds had made him the "head of everything," as Rose liked to say. He was paid a salary of six dollars a week to manage the plantation. He also spent part of his day working in his own fields.

The baby toddled over to Rayford. He bent down, scooped him up, and laughed at the child's plump, dark legs dangling in the air.

"Little Ray walkin' all over the place now, Rosie," Easter said. Jason made faces at the baby, who let out tiny peals of laughter as he sat on his father's lap. While she watched

Jason and Little Ray playing, Easter tried to find the best way to tell Rose and Rayford that she'd be leaving the plantation. It was strangely frightening and exciting to be able to walk off the plantation and do something she'd been planning to do for three years.

There was a tap on the door, and Melissa and Sarah entered. The two women sat down at the large pine table. They all ate together every evening, as they'd done in the old days.

"I hear Mr. Reynolds is coming tomorrow to talk to us," Rayford said. He handed the baby to Jason.

"We'll have our own land soon," said Rose.

Easter hunted for a way to tell them her news. Sarah's voice broke into her thoughts.

"I leavin' tomorrow," Sarah said quietly.

"Leaving? Why?" Rose asked. Easter was surprised also. Sarah had never talked about leaving the plantation before.

"Want to find my husband."

"What were you told at the Freedmen's Bureau?" Rayford asked her.

Sarah's eyes had dark circles under them, making her appear drawn and tired. "They can't help me. I go from place to place till I find him myself." Sarah spoke Easter's thoughts.

"Suppose you don't find him?" Rayford asked. "And the land? You worked hard. If you leave now, you might not get anything."

"I been tellin' her that, Mister Ray," Melissa said.

"I have to go. Melissa can have the acres I been workin'."

Easter reached across the table and patted the woman's hand. "I understand," she said softly.

Rayford glanced at Easter. "Will you be the next one to go?"

He a mind reader, Easter thought. Now that the question was asked, she had to answer. She nodded.

"Oh no, Easter. Not you too. I thought you'd settled

down and had forgot all that business about leavin'," Rose exclaimed.

"I have to find Obi now."

Rose stood up and started taking dishes down off the mantel. Melissa helped her. "But what about the school? You the only teacher the children have."

Easter had been continuing to help the young children with the alphabet and reading simple words. Jason and the older children didn't go to school any longer but worked full time in the fields. Easter didn't have to take care of the babies anymore because Aunt Louise, one of the older field hands who couldn't work in the fields anymore, took care of them. "When the missionary society send a new teacher, then I leavin'."

"Miss Grantley want you to go to the school in Philadelphia. What about that?" Rose asked. "Me and Rayford was even talking about how all of us here on the plantation could raise some money for you to go north. So you could come back here and be our own teacher."

Easter left the table and walked over to the three-legged iron skillet. She appreciated their kindness, but she knew what she wanted. Picking up a bowl from the sideboard, she began to dish out the rice. "After I find Obi, then me and Jason go north."

Jason stopped playing with Little Ray. "I want to be with you, Easter, but I want to be in Dr. Taylor's show."

"What show?" Rose asked.

"That sounds like something you'd want to do," Rayford said, shaking his head, when Jason finished explaining. "The man is probably a scamp. Better stay around your own people and learn how to do something besides sing and dance."

Jason looked dejected, and Easter felt a little sorry for him. "Jason, it won't be so bad. You'll see the other islands, and Mariah and Gabriel. Then we go north," she told him.

"You better get the schooling, then come back down

here and run a school. It could take a long time to find Obi—if you ever do," Rayford said.

"I know how Easter feel, Mister Ray. Her heart never rest easy till she know where her Obi is," Sarah said softly.

Easter smiled gratefully at her. At least someone understood how she felt.

There was another knock on the door. At first Easter didn't recognize the tall young man with the high cheekbones, until he tipped his army cap.

"Julius!" Jason screeched as he leapt up off the floor. He stood stiffly and saluted as he'd seen the soldiers do during drill.

Everyone embraced Julius. Only Easter remained by the iron skillet. He made a good-looking figure in his uniform, and she was glad that he was safely home. "Hello, Julius," she said, smiling. "Glad you back."

"Amen," Rose cried. "And what about the other men from here? They all come back?"

"All except Luther and John. Heard they was sent to Richmond. Been some big battles there."

Suddenly Easter felt cold. Suppose Obi had been in Richmond too? She drove the thought from her mind.

Julius walked over to Easter and hugged her. "You the prettiest thing I seen in a long time."

"Oh, hush." She shyly avoided his eyes.

Rose put another plate on the table. "Eat with us."

"Yes," Rayford said. "There's enough."

Julius sat down next to Sarah. "You don't have to ask twice. You know how many times I dream about home cooking? That Yankee army food taste like straw." Julius talked about his past months in the army, and everyone brought Julius up to date on what was happening on the plantation.

"You're entitled to two acres of land. We worked on your portion for you."

"Thank you. And I save almost every penny I make in

the army, so I can buy some more land to farm and find me a pretty wife."

"Who you want for a wife? Easter?" Jason blurted out.

Easter was embarrassed. "Stay out of grown-up conversation."

Julius rubbed Jason's head. "That's not a bad idea."

"Did you see or hear about Obi?" Easter asked.

"No. Didn't meet up with Obi."

Rose grinned at her. "Easter, Julius look good in them Yankee blues, don't he?"

Easter picked up her fork. "Yes. Bet Obi look good too if he wearin' a uniform." Julius sighed.

Rayford wiped his mouth. "I didn't expect you to be home so soon."

"Them Yankee is musterin' us colored troops out early. Heard they don't want to upset the Rebels by havin' too many of us runnin' 'round here with uniforms and guns. Ain't nothing a Rebel hate more than a colored Union soldier."

The next morning, Easter stood outside of the schoolhouse as usual. She listened to Paul and two other carpenters hammering as they put the finishing touches on the new church building. For a year everyone had been contributing money toward buying the materials for the church.

She heard keys jangling and knew that Rayford was nearby. He waved to her as he passed the cabins. Easter noticed that Paul and the other men were doing more talking and laughing than hammering, and people were coming out of their huts, sauntering to the fields in a relaxed way, as if it were Sunday morning.

However, Virginia, George's wife, ran out of her cabin, calling excitedly after Rayford, "Mister Ray! Mister Ray, come here!" David, Isaiah, and Nathan, looking confused and embarrassed, trailed after their mother.

Easter ran over to her. "What's the matter?"

Virginia seemed not even to hear Easter. Rayford walked

over to the agitated woman. "Mister Ray, that fool husband of mine say he free now and he ain't goin' to work in no fields that he don't have title to."

Easter chuckled and Rayford seemed amused also. He patted Virginia on her shoulder. "Calm down, Ginny. The man's not wrong, now. But the fields your family's been working do belong to you. Mr. Reynolds is coming here this afternoon. I'm sure he's going to talk to us about the land."

"That's what I try to tell George, but he head like stone. You talk to him." Her long thin arms looked like tree branches as she spread them out in frustration.

"Let the man be. He'll work this afternoon. Why don't you and the boys go on to the field?" Rayford jingled his keys as he walked away.

Easter went back to the school, glad that it wasn't an emergency. When she passed the carpenters, she heard Paul say, "George master of his own body now, and his body say it want to rest."

Later that morning, as the children formed the letters of the alphabet on their slates, one of the women peeped inside the classroom. "Mr. Reynolds here!"

"Children, give me your slates," Easter said.

"Miss Easter, I want to stay here," Charlotte protested.

"We'll come back after we hear what Mr. Reynolds has to tell us." She led the children out of the school. Even though she knew that she wouldn't be getting any land, she was excited along with the others.

As she walked toward the big house, she saw Julius with several of the other young men who'd been in the army. Wearing overalls now, they looked like farmers; however, they still wore their army caps. Every resident of the plantation was there—even the house servants, the cook rushing out of the house nervously wiping her hands on her apron, with the butler behind her. Rayford, Brother Thomas, Elijah, and Paul took their places in front of everyone else. Easter sensed a tense mood among the people, a change from the lightness of the morning.

There was a middle-aged white couple and a young white man with Mr. Reynolds. Mr. Reynolds ran his fingers through his hair. "You people have kept this plantation in fine condition. We all thank God that the awful war has ended and now we can heal our wounds." His face grew more flushed with every word he spoke.

The three people standing next to him stared unflinchingly into the crowd. A tiny, sad smile hovered around the woman's mouth. Mr. Reynolds continued speaking, his eyes shifting and moving as if he dared not gaze closely at any of the faces before him. "You people have done yeomen's service. The plantation is in wonderful condition, and the Williams family want to reward your labor."

Easter relaxed. People would get their land.

Mr. Reynolds pointed to the people next to him. "For those of you who do not know, let me introduce Mr. and Mrs. Charles Williams and their son, Richard. The family will pay you fair wages if you remain here and work for them. They will sign contracts for your labor."

The words hung over the crowd like thick storm clouds. At first, Easter thought she'd heard wrong. The shocked silence was as vast as the sky; then voices of people shattered it like the thunder that warns of a storm.

Rayford stood as still as a block of wood. "That's not what you promised us. You promised us that after the war we'd be given the amount of land we tilled, and that we could buy additional acres," he said calmly and slowly and clearly.

"That's right." Brother Thomas pointed an accusing finger at Mr. Reynolds. "You told us that very thing."

The family said nothing.

"I knew it," George yelled at Virginia. "That's why something tell me not to go in them field this morning."

Easter wondered how this could happen. How could a

promise be broken as if it were nothing, as if it were just an old toy?

Mr. Reynolds held up his hand. "The government has changed its policy. Our new president, Mr. Johnson, has ordered that the plantations are to be returned to their original owners. We are healing the wounds of war. Don't you people understand that?" He held his large hands out to them pleadingly. "We are trying to help everyone. Is it fair that this family should lose everything? We are trying to heal wounds. The family will pay you good wages to work for them. You can stay in your homes, and you are free men and women. What more could you ask?"

"We ask that you keep your promise!" Paul shouted.

"We thought we was workin' for the government, not the Williams family," another man added.

"The master and mistress get all their property back except us!" someone yelled.

Everyone talked at once. Easter was as outraged as those who'd toiled in good faith as she gazed at their disappointed and angry faces.

Mr. Reynolds addressed Rayford. "You have done a wonderful job. You're a talented, intelligent fellow who will do well in life. But now I must have the keys to the barns and other buildings so that I can return them to the family." He held out his hand.

Rayford folded his arms, and the other men gathered near him, as if forming a wall. "I ain't returnin' nothing," he spat out. "We had a bargain, and I mean to make you keep it."

Brother Thomas's barrel chest and strong, muscular arms seemed to bulge. He spoke to the Williams family, his former owners. "You ain't gettin' all this land back. This Yankee make a bargain with us," he said, pointing to Mr. Reynolds, "and we holdin' him to it."

A chorus of "Yes! We holdin' him to it" erupted behind Thomas.

Mrs. Williams's cool exterior finally crumbled. "Thomas?

How could you do this? You were one of our best . . ." She broke down in tears and couldn't continue. Her husband ignored her, while the son tried to comfort his mother.

Mr. Reynolds had run his fingers through his hair so many times that it seemed to stand on end. Charles Williams had turned the color of a pomegranate. "All of you will be arrested and whipped," he threatened.

"Calm down, sir," Mr. Reynolds said. "We'll settle this directly." Turning to Rayford again, Mr. Reynolds held out his hand once more. "Give me back those keys, now," he demanded. "You are defying the orders of the United States government."

"We're not giving anything back!" Rayford yelled in a loud rush of words like a dam finally bursting. "Not one boll of cotton, not one cow pea, until we get our land!"

"If we don't get the land we work for, then we leave this plantation an' you lose the whole crop!" Brother Thomas shouted.

"Yes," another man spoke out. "You know all the good people sign contract for the year an' they already workin'. This place be in ruin if we leave now."

One of the young men who'd served with Julius in the army yelled, "If you don't agree to give us the land, I burnin' down everything 'fore I go. Won't have to worry about crops then."

Another man agreed with the ex-soldier. "Yes, we burn the place down like the good General Sherman done." Mr. Reynolds and the Williams family grew pale.

The crowd moved forward. Paul stepped in front of Rayford and stood nose to nose with Mr. Reynolds. "Y'all best leave. Bad for your health if you stay here."

Easter saw fear in the faces of Mr. Reynolds and the family as they headed quickly toward the plantation gates. Suddenly, the butler jumped out of the crowd and ran after the quickly retreating whites. "I ain't part of this, Massa. I ain't with these crazy people. I still want to be with you."

CHAPTER

TWELVE

The great cry of our people is to have land.

Tunis Campbell, ex-slave

Easter was numb from the shock of what had happened. How could the government, or whoever made the rules, change things and hurt people who trusted it? She rubbed her throbbing forehead as she followed the others to their old meeting place behind the stables. "This ain't over yet," Julius warned. "They be back."

"How many of you men are willin' to make them give us our due?" asked one of the men who'd been in the army with Julius.

"We stay and fight."

"Don't give up the keys, Mister Ray."

"You did the right thing, Mister Ray."

Easter listened. *Yes, keep them keys,* she said to herself.

An older man shook his gray head as he sat down slowly on a log. "I don't feel right takin' old Master and Mistress lands. I movin' to Elenaville."

Brother Thomas slapped his fist in his open palm and faced the man. "Who been in them field working for nothin' all these many years? Tell me that. We ain't askin' for all the pies, just the ones we baked. Me and my family work ten acres. That's all I askin' for. What's the sense in bein' free if you don't have nothing? What kind of freedom is that, fool?" His eyes looked as if they would pop out of his head as he leaned into the man's face. He lost his breath for a moment. Anna rushed to his side, patting him on the back.

But the cook, her hands on her hips, disagreed. "This ain't none of our place. I want to stay here and work for Mistress like I use to do." She glared at Rose. "That cottage you been livin' in use to be mine 'fore I move to the big house. Now that my mistress is return I movin' back to my cottage."

Rayford swung around. "You ain't moving nowhere!" he shouted.

Another woman tapped the cook on the shoulder. "What you goin' to tell your mistress about them clothes you been sellin'?"

"This ain't no time for us to be fussin' with each other," Paul yelled at both of the women. "Those of you who want to stay and work for the Williams family, that's your business, but don't get in our way."

Easter and Jason held hands. He pulled her toward him so that he could whisper in her ear. "Easter, let's go look for Obi now. I don't want to stay here."

She squeezed his hand. "We will Jason. Soon as the new teacher come."

The cook and the old man walked away from the rest of the group. "I goin' to Elenaville," he mumbled. "This is Master and Mistress land."

"We leavin' too, Rayford," George announced. "I takin' my family and the money we save and we leavin'."

"Don't give up now, man," Rayford said. "You and your family worked three years for this land."

There were tears in Virginia's eyes as she followed her husband and sons toward the huts. One of the ex-soldiers said, "We have to figure out what's going to happen next, people, 'fore they come back."

"Maybe they send in patterollers," someone suggested.

"No. We under the authority of the army. Ain't no

authority now except the Union army, so we—"Julius stopped short as if something had hit him. "The army. They could send in the army."

"They wouldn't do that," Brother Thomas said. "The army free us."

Rayford's face seemed as hard as stone. "We don't know what they'll do, so we have to be prepared for anything. Those of us from the Phillips plantation have rifles and shotguns."

Brother Thomas sat on a log, his breathing still labored and heavy. "Master Williams had many gun in the house, but the Yankee take those when they first come here. Some of us have shotgun and rifle."

Julius put his hands in the pocket of his overalls. "We all brought back guns from the war."

Easter felt as frightened as she had when she'd run away from the Confederate camp. She prayed that there wouldn't be any shooting or fighting.

That night, Rose and the baby slept in the cabin with Melissa and Easter. The other families who lived in the cottages moved out, and all the women and children stayed in the quarters. If there was any shooting, they would be safer there. The men slept in the cottages in order to be close to the big house and the gates. They figured that anyone entering the plantation would come that way rather than from the woods. Several men stayed in the area of the huts to protect the women and children, and a few men were posted at the edge of the woods as a precaution.

Only the children slept soundly. The heavens opened up that night, and it stormed. "This rain may be a good sign, Rosie. Nobody come here in a storm," Easter said.

Rose watched Little Ray sleeping contentedly with Jason. "I think Mr. Reynolds come tomorrow with a passel of talk. But we standin' fast. Nothing happen. Don't worry, Easter," she said.

Easter wasn't so sure that nothing would happen. All

night she was startled awake by the slightest noise. When she finally dozed off to sleep, chirping birds woke her up.

Melissa sat by the door, her rifle in her hands. Although it was a weekday, the fields were empty except for the growing cotton plants; even the animals clung close to the gates. Everyone remained indoors, waiting. They waited through the misty, rainy, still morning.

Later on in the morning, however, the sun burned off the mist. The magnolia trees had finished blooming, but roses wound around the open latticework that shaded the veranda of the big house. Robins and blue-green swallows flew in the sunshine. The people of the Williams plantation waited for something to happen.

Finally, the crack of a firearm ended the waiting. Melissa sprung to the door and stuck the nose of her rifle through the slight opening. There was another crack and then rapid firing, coming from the direction of the big house.

Easter, Jason, and Rose, with Little Ray on her lap, huddled in a corner. Easter covered her ears, imagining all of the men being killed. Jason's eyes were huge with fright. Rose rocked Little Ray, who began to whimper. They'd hear shouts and then weapons firing and then silence. Even the birds had stopped singing. When it seemed to Easter that she couldn't stand being confined and not knowing what was happening a moment longer, she heard a tap on the shutter. "Me—Julius. Open up."

Melissa let him in. "Rose," was all he said. He walked over to her, and Easter could see in his eyes that something terrible had happened.

Rose knew too. Her large, round eyes filled with tears. She pulled at Julius's sleeve. "Rayford?" she whispered hoarsely. "Something happen?"

"Rayford been shot, Rosie. He . . . he dead."

Rose closed her eyes and let out a long, low moan. Easter and Melissa both held the sobbing woman in their arms; then Easter left Rose with Melissa and walked over to

Julius, who stood by the door. He had puffy bags under his eyes.

"How it happen?" she asked him.

"The army come."

"Rebels?"

"Union, Easter. They ain't no more Rebel army."

She shook her head as she tried to hold back the tears that wanted to pour out. "I didn't think the Yankee would bring in the army. Why, Julius? Why? How Rayford get . . ." She began to sob.

Julius wiped her face with his fingers. "The soldiers come through the entrance. They seem skittish when they didn't see nobody. We was in the cottages. They kicked open the door of Rayford's cottage. We hear shootin'—don't know who fire first. I see a couple of soldiers on the ground, and Rayford, Brother Thomas, Samuel, Elijah, and James on the ground with them. They been shot too, but not as bad as Rayford."

Suddenly, Rose dashed out of the hut and ran toward the cottages. Easter called after her, "It ain't safe, Rose."

"The soldiers gone," Julius said, "but they'll be back with more men. They didn't come with too many this first time."

Easter walked over to Jason, who held the whimpering Little Ray tightly. "I scared," he said, "but I tryin' to play happy to keep Little Ray from crying."

"Don't be afraid," she said, hating her own words. He was right to be afraid. "I goin' to Rose's. You stay here with the baby and Melissa. You actin' like a real little man, Jason. Things clear up soon." Her shaky voice belied her words.

Easter ran to the cottages. As she neared the buildings she saw the cook waddling down the steps of the big house. She carried two large bundles and wore a dark blue traveling suit. "Y'all is crazy," she yelled at the men, moving as fast as she could down the road.

Julius and the other ex-soldiers had taken charge and

were trying to organize everyone. Paul was in the house with Rayford.

"The rest of you men go near the woods. You women stay in the quarters. The army will be back," Julius warned.

"How you going to fight the whole army?" a woman asked. Her thick eyebrows met as she scowled at Julius. "They beat up the Rebels—what you think they do to us?"

"That's right," Anna added tearfully as she crouched over Brother Thomas. "Look at all these men hurt. And Mister Ray dead."

"Woman, shut up and get them wounded men to the quarters," Elias shouted.

"Don't tell her to shut up. We women has a right to say something too," Mary shouted back at Elias. "We need doctors, not more fighting."

Another man tried to calm her. "There'll be more fighting. Go on back to the quarters and help them sick men."

Easter's body was drenched with sweat as she strained to help Anna get Brother Thomas to his feet. Julius came over and helped them pull him up. Thomas moaned in pain from his leg and arm wounds.

"We fix you up," Anna said as Thomas put one arm around Easter's shoulders and the other around her. His blood dripped down Easter's arm. She felt as if she would collapse under the big man's weight, yet she struggled with Brother Thomas and concentrated now only on helping the wounded.

Brother Thomas opened his mouth, which was slightly twisted, but no sound came out.

"Dear Jesus," Anna cried, "he can't talk."

Julius held Brother Thomas's face. "Say something," he begged.

Thomas only grunted and cried in pain. One of the women helped another man get up. "We takin' these wounded men to the cottage," she said. "We can't drag them to no quarters."

Samuel held his hands up in resignation. "Y'all women hardhead."

Rose's cottage became an infirmary. Rose, Isabel, Paul, and the woman who took care of the children, Aunt Louise, were in the bedroom with Rayford. Easter and Anna cleaned Brother Thomas's wounds, and then Easter helped with the rest of the injured men. She held one man's hand while one of the women took a bullet out of his arm with a knife.

Rose walked into the kitchen with the keys in her hand. "This what he die for—this," she said, throwing the keys onto the table.

Easter sat down next to Rose at the table. Suddenly, everything Rayford had been trying to tell her over the past several years made sense. "He ain't die for no keys, Rose, he die for the land. And because he a man. Men fight and die for what they believe in. Like the war, Rose."

Rose covered her face with her hands and tears trickled between her fingers. "Do it make sense to keep fightin' when you know you can't win? What's the sense in all us bein' dead?" Rose's voice was muffled by her hands.

Easter watched the four injured men. *How can we win and keep on living too? That's what we have to find out.* She put her arms around Rose as she turned the question over and over in her mind. *Do we always have to fight and die?*

Rose picked up the keys. "I make sure Rayford get he land."

Easter stood up. "Rose, you sit and rest while I help the others."

But Rose stood up too. "I have to keep busy. Aunt Louise an' Isabel getting Rayford ready to bury," Rose said. "I make some tea, Easter."

Easter went outside to throw away the dirty water and get a fresh supply. She walked to the well near the cottages. The men were still ordering frightened women and children back to the quarters. When she finished drawing the water, Easter saw the young black man who worked as a courier for Mr. Reynolds. She hurriedly took the water inside and rushed back to find out what the messenger wanted.

He had ridden through the gates on a horse, waving a big white shirt on a stick. His hands shook nervously now as they clutched the reins. Easter joined the rest of the crowd that rushed over to the messenger. "Who runnin' things here?" he asked.

Julius strode up to the messenger. He handed Julius an envelope, and Julius quickly opened it and removed a letter. He stared at it a moment. Easter could tell by the way he stared at the paper that he couldn't read. She went to his side. "I try read it for you, Julius," she said. He gave her the note.

The powerful plantation grapevine system still worked. Someone raced to the men who'd been posted near the woods and told them that Mr. Reynolds's messenger was there. More of the women left the quarters when they saw the men running from the woods. The children stayed with Melissa and the few women who remained in the huts. Even Isabel and Aunt Louise left the cottage.

Elias was waving his arms at everyone. "Get back to the woods. You women go back to the quarters!" The women ignored him.

Easter watched the people running from the woods and the quarters. "Go on, read the note," Julius ordered.

"I waitin' for the rest. They comin', so they might as well hear it too."

"That's right, daughter," Aunt Louise said. "This note for all of us."

When everyone was assembled, there was a hush as Easter read in a soft, halting voice.

Dear Rayford,

We do not wish to have any further bloodshed or to hurt you people, but you are willfully disobeying government orders and have created a state of insurrection. The Williams family, however, will discuss other terms that we think will be quite agreeable and fair. If we do not receive an answer within the half hour, we have no choice but to move you out forcibly.

Emerson Reynolds

There was a momentary hush. Paul's hammering as he made Rayford's coffin was the only sound.

Aunt Louise spoke out first. "Tell them we talk to them. We can't fight the army," she said.

Julius shouted her down. "No! Ain't nothing to talk about. They just cheat us again."

"How we beat them?" a woman screamed.

They yelled back and forth. Easter stood there, holding the letter limply at her side, the question surging through her mind, as well. *How can we get what we want without getting hurt?*

"The superintendent want an answer right away," the messenger shouted. "Y'all better tell him something before they send the army in here again." His small eyes seemed to do a nervous waltz in his head.

Julius glanced at Easter. "Our schoolteacher will answer the letter, and she will say that we will not give up. We demand our land."

A woman pointed to the cottages. "Rayford in there dead, and other mens is hurt. Easter will send a message sayin' we goin' to discuss this problem."

The men and women continued to argue back and forth—most of the women not wanting to continue fighting. The messenger leaned over his horse toward Easter. "Miss, you better hurry and answer that note. This the United States army these people foolin' with."

"What you waitin' for, Easter?" one of the men asked, glaring at her. "Write a note tellin' Reynolds that we ain't talkin'. This just some more of their tricks."

"That's what you and some of these men sayin', but that's not what these women sayin'," Easter told him.

Gregory, one of the ex-soldiers who'd been in the army

with Julius, snatched the letter out of her hand. "You ain't the only one who can read and write. I'll answer this note." He *ran* up the steps of the big house in order to get paper and pen. The women yelled after him.

Easter turned to the messenger. "Wait. I be back with a note." She *dashed* to the quarters with the women following her. *Hope I can write faster than him,* she thought.

"The first note I get, I takin'," the messenger yelled after them.

Easter rushed into her cabin. A few children had joined Jason and Little Ray inside. The women explained to the surprised Melissa what had happened, as Easter took a wooden stationery box out of her basket. The box held the paper, pen, and ink that Miss Grantley had given her so that they could correspond. Easter wrote quickly, hoping that Gregory was still searching for pen and paper:

Dear Mr. Reynolds,
    We will talk to you. Do not shoot us anymore.
                            The People of the Williams
                            Plantation

Easter read the note to them quickly and hurried to the messenger. She was relieved to see that he was still there, steadying his horse, which pranced nervously. She reached him and handed him the note just as Gregory ran down the steps of the big house and the women had caught up to Easter.

"Wait," he shouted to the messenger.

The messenger hesitated.

"Go on!" Easter said firmly. "We don't need no more shootin' and killin' in here." He turned his horse around and left.

"Where you going? Come back!" Gregory shouted.

The women faced the men. "We give him the note. We tell Mr. Reynolds that we discuss this problem," Easter said.

"Who give you the right to speak for us?" Gregory asked.

Easter spread her arms to include the other women. "Is what we decide. Not me alone."

"We give her the right," Anna said as the women drew closer to Easter. "We don't want fighting."

Julius frowned. "What did you say?" Easter repeated the gist of her reply.

"You had no business to say that!" the ex-soldier said in a rage.

The women bore down on him. "We say no more fight, so there be no more fight."

Elias calmed the men. "It done. You men know we can't win no battle with the whole army."

Easter walked toward the cottages. She felt drained now, and her head throbbed. Aunt Louise put her arms around Easter. "Thank you, daughter," she said softly.

"Wish all this trouble was over," Easter said.

The old woman smiled sadly. "Trouble never over. Just have to learn how to ride it, like you ride a wild horse."

CHAPTER
THIRTEEN

For we are all ready in the boat, and they seek to cast us in the sea.

> Sam Aleckson, ex-slave
> *Before the War and After the Union*

Easter left the cottage the next morning as Mr. Reynolds walked through the gates of the plantation, accompanied by several soldiers. Everyone else had already gathered in front of the big house. Julius had told her a few minutes before the superintendent's arrival that a regiment was waiting farther down the road in case there was trouble.

She heard her own heart pounding as she prayed that the people would get something for all of their hard work. Rose stood next to her, a dull, faraway look in her eyes. Jason and some of the other children sat under the dogwood trees near the big house. He watched Little Ray for Rose.

Mr. Reynolds stepped before the crowd. "First, let me tell you that I am sorry that Rayford is dead. We didn't intend for anything like that to happen. The family wishes me to inform you that they regret the bloodshed. They want to make amends."

"We don't want to hear all that," Gregory called out. "What about our land?"

The superintendent's large hands trembled as he took a piece of paper from his inside pocket and put on his spectacles. "The Williams family," he read, "will sell you fifteen hundred acres of their land, in fifty-acre plots at ten dollars an acre. You will also be given the amount of acreage that you cultivated this year. Your acreage and the land for sale will be the unused land beginning at the edge of the woods."

Easter gazed past the pastures and the cultivated fields toward the thick woods. "It's goin' to be a lot of work clearing that land," she whispered to Rose.

Mr. Reynolds continued. "You will receive the free land based on the amount of crops you bring in at the end of this year."

"Wait a minute, wait a minute." Elias waved his hands excitedly while everyone else talked and murmured. "You mean, if we work five acre other years but only four acre this year, then we receive four acre?"

"I'm afraid so. That's the way it has to be—based on this year's work."

"That's not fair!" Elias shouted.

Tempers and voices began to rise. About a dozen people left. "Let the massa pick he own cotton," one said angrily. "I gone."

Julius faced the group. "Quiet folks, maybe this ain't so bad. Some people only work two and three acres. Now that we know we gettin' this land, you could work more."

"An' I hear that some of the people on Riverside plantation try to buy land and nobody would sell to them. This may be the only way for us to get a piece of earth," Aunt Louise said.

"How we know that we get our land?" Paul asked Mr. Reynolds.

"You have our word."

"Your word change like the wind."

They forgetting to ask for the one important thing, Easter said to herself. She stepped closer to the front, where Mr. Reynolds could see her. "We have to have this promise in writing," she said, surprised at the firmness of her own voice.

A chorus of shouts went up behind her. "Yes, yes, Easter. That's right."

Then it was Rose's turn. "And we not givin' up these keys until we get the land."

There was another chorus of shouts. Mr. Reynolds raised his hands for order. "There will be an agreement drawn up. However, if you do not keep your part of the bargain you will receive no land, either as a gift or to buy."

Samuel, stooped and with his arm in a sling, walked slowly up to Mr. Reynolds. "Excuse me, suh, but all that land we gettin' has to be cleared. The family's keepin' the land we been cultivatin'. But we go along with the plan. Have no choice. Main thing is we get some land and have the chance to buy more. But we want you to know that we know that this ain't no Christmas gift."

They all clapped in agreement with Samuel. Easter had never heard him say so much at one time. Julius spoke quietly to her. "Mr. Reynolds messenger is here, and he tell me that the family owe money to people all over the state. That's why they sellin' this land. This way they make money instead of losin' their land to people they owe. Samuel be about right."

Rayford was buried that evening at the edge of the woods, where their lands would begin. When the funeral ended, people went to Rose and Rayford's cottage to offer Rose their condolences. People came and went all evening. Rose's eyes reflected her pain, even though her mouth tried to smile. Easter knew that there was little that she could say to Rose to make her feel better, so she sat quietly near her all evening as Jason and Little Ray lay curled on the pallet in front of the fireplace, fast asleep. Finally, Easter and Aunt Louise were the only visitors still there. "Rose, don't go tryin' to work all them fields by yourself," Aunt Louise said.

"Auntie, I use to field work now. I make do."

Easter hadn't even thought of that. Now that the granting of land would be based on this year's work, Rose could lose the land that Rayford had been cultivating.

Aunt Louise stood up stiffly, rubbing her leg. "Daughter, you can't do all that work alone. It impossible."

When the old woman left, Rose turned to Easter. "You and Jason sleep here tonight. I don't want me and Little Ray to be alone."

Easter rose with the birds and slipped out of the cottage the following morning. She rushed to her hut as the sun was rising. Melissa was still sleeping. Easter got her pen, ink, and a sheet of paper and sat at the table. She began to write rapidly.

My Dear Miss Grantley,

I have made a decision. I will never go to the North. The Yankees, except for you, are awful people. I cannot live among them. This is a very sad story that I have to tell you, then you will know why I will stay here for the rest of my life.

Easter told Miss Grantley what had happened. She'd send Jason to the general store later so that he could mail the letter. She then tiptoed quietly to her bed and changed to her old field dress, which was now too snug and too short. She wrapped her head in an old piece of blue cloth, took off her slippers, and left the hut.

The sky was a pale pink, and the clean morning air smelled of flowers and pine. Easter was pleased with her decisions as she ran to the cottage. She started a fire so that she could prepare grits for their breakfast. Little Ray and Jason still slept.

Rose walked into the kitchen wearing her field apron over her shift and carrying her straw hat. She frowned when she saw Easter.

"Where your schoolteacher dress and your slippers? Why you dress like that? And barefoot."

"School close until a new teacher come."

Rose rested her hat on the rocking chair. "I thought you was the teacher until then."

"Maybe I teach Sunday School. Remember Brother Thomas say the children should have a Sunday School? I give them reading then." She poured the grits into the boiling water as Rose stared at her incredulously. "I going to help you. Me and some of my students help you bring in the crop from Rayford field so you get all the land he work for."

"Easter, I can't ask you to—"

"You didn't ask."

"No, Easter. The children need school. And you know how you hate field work. I manage."

"Tell me who love field work? Yes, I hate it, and I will always hate it."

Rose took the dishes off the mantel. "Don't you worry about me. I get that land Rayford work for."

Easter put her hands on her hips and faced Rose. "Rosie, you couldn't make me stay in them fields when I didn't want to, and you can't keep me out if I want to help you."

In June Easter received a letter from Miss Grantley:

My Dear Easter,

I was very disturbed by the terrible news. I do not in any way blame you for feeling the way you do. I too am ashamed at the way some of my fellow citizens have comported themselves.

Easter, one of the greatest lessons of our sojourn on earth is that we must not let the wrongdoings of a few people cause us to become bitter ourselves. There are many good people in the Northern Missionary Society who want to help you.

Please do not close your mind to ever coming north and continuing your studies. It would be a loss to the numerous students who will not receive the gift of your love.

I have some further news. A new teacher will be coming to the plantation in September to continue the school. She is a wonderful young colored woman who graduated from the Philadelphia School for Colored Youth.

I know that you will welcome her and help her to settle in. Easter, please think about your decision and reconsider.

With Much Affection,
Amy Grantley

Easter read the letter twice. She was always happy to get a letter from Miss Grantley, but her mind was set. Miss Grantley didn't understand. Easter couldn't forget the day the Union soldiers rode onto the plantation. She couldn't forget Rayford or Brother Thomas, who still could not speak. She folded the letter and put it away, glad that the children would be getting a real teacher.

As Easter walked toward the cotton fields, she closed her mind to Miss Grantley's letter and advice, having learned how to shut her mind like a door when she worked in the fields. The only thing that she reminded herself of was her promise to help Rose keep the land.

CHAPTER
FOURTEEN

Had my first regular teaching experience . . . it was not a very pleasant one. Part of my scholars are very tiny . . . it is hard to keep them quiet and interested while I am hearing the larger ones. They are too young even for the alphabet.

The Journal of Charlotte Forten
Teacher, 1862–1864, Port Royal, South Carolina

September 1865

The cotton bolls began to blanket the fields. Easter and Jason, with sacks hanging from their shoulders, picked the soft, white bolls. Jason worked a few feet ahead of Easter. She noticed that he'd grown a little taller and fuller without her knowing when it happened. He'd been unusually quiet too for the past four months. *Still thinkin' about Rayford and what happened,* she supposed. *Nobody been feeling too right.* Usually Jason kept up a stream of chatter while he worked, and when he was tired of talking, he'd sing, sometimes songs he'd made up himself.

When she and Jason stopped to eat lunch, Jason ate with her instead of sitting with the other youngsters. They found a shady spot under a tree at the edge of the fields.

"When you goin' back to the Bureau?" Jason asked.

"Never. No sense goin' back there. They can't help me find Obi."

"When you leavin' here? Thought you want to find Obi so bad and leave here?"

"When Rose get settle with her land, we go and look for Obi. I glad you want to find him too." She took a bite of cornbread.

"I want to leave, Easter. I hate these field. I hope you find Obi soon."

"What? You comin' with me, Jason."

"I want to go with Dr. Taylor."

"Who?"

"The man with the show, remember?"

"Jason, I thought you forget all that. Suppose that man is evil?"

"Then I leave him and come back."

Easter stared at Jason, seeing for the first time that he was losing his baby face and beginning to look like a young man. He ate his rice slowly and seemed to be deep in thought. Suddenly he said, "You remember my real mother?"

She was surprised. He'd never asked about his mother before. "I tell you while we work. Make the time go fast."

People were heading back to the fields. A flock of sea gulls flew toward the ocean. They picked up their sacks and walked back to the cotton fields. Jason worked steadily as Easter related her story. "You beginnin' to look like your ma. She was pretty, and our old mistress like her a lot. . . ."

While they ate supper that evening, Paul, who now managed the plantation, visited them.

"Paul," Rose greeted him, "have supper with us."

He sat down, and stretched his legs out before him. "No thanks, Rosie. Just come to bring you good news. We get a letter from the missionaries." He handed Easter the letter. "You can read it. They sendin' us a teacher is what it say. And I want you to go to the ferry landing in Elenaville to meet her, since you been our teacher when we had none."

So a week later Easter, dressed in her good violet dress and her worn brown leather slippers, waited at the plantation gates for James to bring the carriage around. They were going to meet the ferry that was carrying Miss Emmaline Fortune, their new teacher. She'd traveled by train from Philadelphia to Charleston and would continue on to Santa Elena by ferry.

Although it was early Saturday morning, Easter heard hammering in the forest. The men were at work clearing the land that would soon be theirs. The first building would be a church and the next a school. She heard James's rickety carriage approaching the gate. He'd purchased the carriage from a planter who was selling his lands and other property. James provided carriage service to the blacks in the area. They didn't use the regular carriage line because either the drivers wouldn't stop for black passengers or there'd be a fight between blacks and whites before they reached their destination. For short trips James still used his mules and wagon.

Easter was glad James arrived before Jason woke up and discovered she was going to Elenaville. When the carriage pulled up, she was surprised to see Julius jump out. "Miss Easter, I joinin' you on your trip. A lady shouldn't travel alone."

"Well, what James be? A ghost?" she asked as he helped her into the carriage.

"James have to worry with them old horses. See that they get us there." Six other people were already in the carriage, which wasn't supposed to hold more than that comfortably.

Easter squeezed in beside a heavy-hipped woman. "Julius, if you stay, then we have more room."

"Can't let you go alone." He smiled playfully, squeezing in beside her.

As soon as they started off down the road, the heavy woman popped out of her seat like a cork out of a bottle. A thin little man sitting next to her was almost knocked down. "Mercy, what caught you?" he asked.

"Something's alive under this seat! James!" she yelled out of the window.

Easter was getting angry with James and Julius—Julius for taking up needed space and James for piling people in the carriage so that he could make as much money as possible. Julius checked the seat as the woman leaned out of the window, still yelling for James. "You should be paying *us* to ride in this thing," she shouted.

Julius found the culprit—a spring poking out of the leather.

"Seem like she have enough rump back there to cushion that," the woman across from Easter whispered.

That school teacher goin' back to Philadelphia if we take her home in this confusion, Easter thought.

James stopped the carriage, and the woman got out and climbed up to sit next to him. Easter was relieved; she carefully stayed away from the lively spring.

They reached Elenaville and went straight to the dock. While James fed his horses, Easter found a shady spot under a live oak tree. Julius walked over to her and sat down. "Easter," he said, flashing a wide smile, "there's something I want to ask you."

She knew what was coming. He'd been buzzing around her ever since he'd come home from the army.

"I want you to marry me, Easter. I a hardworking man, not like some of these lazy scamps."

She sighed and stared at her scratched hands. "I have to find Obi."

"Where you findin' him? Why you not lookin' for him now?"

"I helpin' Rose. I can't look for him yet."

"I wonder if he tryin' to find you?" Julius's face was serious now, the high cheekbones sharp and slightly glistening with moisture.

"He is lookin' for me."

"Don't you want your own family? A real family?"

"Obi and Jason my family."

"Jason not your child. How about your own child, and me for a husband? And a farm we all own. How about that?"

It made sense. What a woman should want. But suppose she did marry Julius and then Obi came for her? "Julius, I have to finish helping Rose, then I find Obi." She kept staring at her hands.

"You and me alike," he continued. "Ain't got no ma, no pa, no real kin and no memory of none." He placed his hand over hers. She let her hands remain under his for a moment—at first it felt strange sitting there like that with Julius. When it began to seem not so strange, she removed her hands.

"Easter, I want a wife."

He was one of the best young men on the plantation; she owned nothing and had no one. But Obi's face clouded her vision.

"Easter, don't give me no answer now. Think on it—but don't think too long."

She had to try and explain how she felt. "Julius, I—"

He touched her lips lightly with his hand. "Don't say nothing till you think on it. Don't want you to tell me no on such a pretty day."

Easter tried to put Julius's offer out of her head as they waited for the ferry, but the war in her mind was beginning. Since she wasn't going north and had no land or anything, maybe . . .

They spotted the ferry approaching the dock. Easter, Julius, and James concentrated on the passengers disembarking. "All I see is white peoples," James remarked.

Easter saw her first. She noticed the gray silk traveling suit with a gray hat to match. Then she saw that the lady wearing the outfit was not white but was a light-brown-skinned young woman who looked confused and a little nervous. "There she is." Easter pointed, ignoring James's "How you know?"

Easter was embarrassed by the way James stared at the

woman with his mouth hanging open. She poked him with her elbow. "She think you a dunce, James."

They walked quickly toward the young woman. James was the first to speak. With a large swooping gesture he took off his battered straw hat, placed it against his chest, and almost bowed to the ground. "We happy to welcome you here, miss."

She smiled sweetly, "Excuse me, sir, what did you say?"

Easter was surprised that she sounded exactly like a Yankee. Julius bowed and said something, which the woman still seemed not to understand. Easter arranged the words in her mind the way Miss Grantley had taught her how to say them.

"Good evening, are you Miss Fortune?"

The woman nodded.

"We from—we are from the Williams plantation, and we come to carry you there. My name's Easter, and these two are Julius and James."

"I'm pleased to meet all of you." She smiled warmly, especially at Easter.

There were no passengers on the return trip, so they could all stretch out. Easter made sure that Miss Fortune didn't sit on the seat with the broken spring.

When they returned to the plantation, everyone was there to welcome the new teacher. Jason ran up to them excitedly. "Easter, why didn't you tell me you was going to Elenaville?" he shouted.

"Jason, don't be rude. Say hello to Miss Fortune, our new teacher."

Jason bowed. "Good evening, Miss Fortune, I so please to meet you. Now, Easter, why you—"

Rose tried to snatch him. "Stop actin' the fool, Jason," she said as she handed the teacher a basket of fruit and pies.

"What a welcome," Miss Fortune exclaimed. "I didn't expect this."

Rose and Easter helped the teacher settle into Rose's old

cottage. Rose had moved out of the cottage and back to the quarters with Melissa and Easter. "I can't live in that house without Rayford," she'd told Easter. Miss Fortune looked around the kitchen as they entered the cottage, which Rose and Isabel had cleaned. Easter hoped that the teacher liked it.

"This is fine. Clean and cozy," Miss Fortune said.

"The bedroom is that way, miss," said Rose. "I have to go and see about my little boy."

"I go now too and let you rest. Charlotte, one of your students, comin' here tomorrow to fix breakfast for you." Easter wasn't in a hurry to leave, but she thought it only polite to do so.

"Do you have to go too, Easter? It would be nice to have company while I unpack." Miss Fortune's brown eyes were slightly slanted and looked soft and kind.

"Oh yes, ma'am. I'll help you," Easter said, picking up one of the bags and carrying it to the bedroom. Easter wondered what other wonderful dresses Miss Fortune had tucked away in her suitcases.

"You don't have to do anything. I just want your company. I want to change into something simpler." Easter tried not to stare as Miss Fortune changed her suit.

She knew that it was rude to stare, but while the teacher struggled to pull a plaid dress over her head, Easter had the chance to get a good look at her bloomers. She'd never seen such fancy underwear, so much lace and ribbon. Easter was suddenly ashamed of her own violet homespun dress and her old slippers.

"Easter, was that perky young fellow your brother?" Miss Fortune asked as she hung up her traveling suit.

"No ma'am," Easter said politely, wondering how many sets of such underwear the teacher owned.

"He seems so close to you."

"We been together since he was a baby."

Miss Fortune hung up another dress. "How did that come to be?"

Easter told Miss Fortune her story. The teacher listened intently as if she were hearing a strange and adventurous tale. When Easter finished, Miss Fortune said, "You're a smart, resourceful young woman. Miss Grantley told me about you when she wrote to me after she learned that I was coming down here." She sat down on the bed next to Easter. "You should be continuing your education."

"I never want to live with the Yankee, Miss Fortune. It's bad enough with these buckra down here."

"What?"

"That's the word we have for the whites who live here—buckra."

"Oh, I see." She twisted her hands and her soft brown eyes took on a faraway look. "I am lucky. My grandfather was a freeman who became wealthy in the sailing business. We have never been slaves, nor have we ever been poor. Yet I still suffer scorn because of my color. And many of my northern colored brethren, especially if they are poor, suffer as greatly as you do in these newly freed states." She stared closely at Easter. "Education is our only weapon against such ignorance. The missionary society sincerely wants to help students such as you. Getting an education is a necessity for colored folks. We have so much work to do."

Miss Emmaline Fortune became an important part of Easter's life. She spent most Saturday and Sunday evenings in the teacher's combination kitchen and sitting room, practicing her reading and writing, remembering how much she missed school. Easter was still torn between her dreams of being with Obi, her wish to study, and Julius's steady proposals of marriage. Only in the quiet of Miss Fortune's cottage was she truly at peace.

By the end of the year much of their land had been cleared, and thirty families purchased fifteen hundred acres of land and received the portions of land that they'd earned. Their Christmas and Emancipation Day celebrations included rejoicing over their success in obtaining land. Yet there was a tinge of sadness as people remembered Rayford and watched the silent Brother Thomas, who had not regained his speech.

Cabins were built by teams of men and boys from the various families working together. Another year of planting, growing, and harvesting ended. The Williams family, along with the cook, butler, and one or two other loyal servants, moved back to the big house. More changes were in the offing.

CHAPTER
FIFTEEN

I've known rivers:
I've known rivers ancient as the world and older than the
flow of human blood in human veins.
My soul has grown deep like the rivers.

Langston Hughes

January 1, 1866
Easter and Rose talked quietly at the pine table while Little
Ray, Melissa, and Jason slept. They'd just finished celebrating Emancipation Day, and Rose and Easter were having
their nightly cup of tea before going to bed.

"Easter, now I have the seven acres me and Rayford work
for—thanks to you—plus the farm I buyin'. I givin' you
two acres."

"I don't want anything, Rosie. I work those field to help
you, not to get land."

"I didn't ask what you want, I tellin' you what I givin'.
Finish lookin' for Obi now, if you have to, but you know
you have somewhere to live. We sisters, even though we
don't have the same mama or papa."

"You still need help, you know," Easter said.

Rose waved her hand. "I have Virginia and George to
help me with the farm. Easter, I think you should go on up
to that Philadelphia school or marry Julius. Don't spend
your whole life lookin' for something that ain't there."

Easter took a sip of tea. "When I think of Virginia an' George that make me really not want to go north."

Virginia, George, and their sons had gotten as far north as Richmond and had to return to the plantation hungry and destitute. "We can't find work in the cities, not enough for a family, and there's the black codes, so you ain't free to go where you want and do what you want. It no different from slavery times," George had said.

Easter sometimes felt as if she were in a tiny box. When she was with Miss Fortune, she felt that she should finish school. Then when she saw Julius working hard with the other men, building a cabin, she thought that maybe she should marry and raise her own family. Then she'd think of Obi.

Rose interrupted her thoughts. "You know, seem like if Obi was lookin' for you, he'd have found you by now."

"How? How he find me, Rose?"

"Seems to me he'd go to the Bureau like you been doin'. That's all he have to do."

"I know he's lookin' for me."

"Well, Easter, Miss Fortune is a nice woman, but it wouldn't be like havin' you for our real teacher. You one of us—sometime Miss Fortune too much like a Yankee woman. She ain't stayin' down here forever." Rose fastened her eyes on Easter. "Well, I guess you goin' to be in them fields forever, though, waitin' for Obi. But you know, things change anyhow, even though we don't even do nothing."

The next morning Easter and Jason picked the last of the cotton. Easter walked over to the sheet spread at the edge of the field and dumped the bolls on it to dry in the sun a bit before one of the children carried the full sheet to the cotton house. Stretching her arms and gazing toward the orchards, she saw a tall figure in a black suit and a large black slouch hat. As he drew closer, she saw that the man had a full, brown mustache. Suddenly Jason raced from the field and took off toward the man. Easter ran behind Jason as he yelled, "Dr. Taylor!"

Oh no, Easter said to herself, *Jason lose his wits now.*

Dr. Taylor smiled, removing his hat and bowing in her direction. "Girlie, I come to ask if the little chap could travel with me for a spell."

"Please, Easter? Let me go," Jason asked before she could answer the man. "I write to you. And I be good, Easter."

As she watched Jason, she remembered everything. His life flashed before her—his mother, his birth, the years they'd spent together, the way he cried when she and Obi left him. Now he was almost a man, wanting to leave—twelve years old, no longer a baby. She had to let go.

"Easter, I come back to see you. I write, and we never be apart the way we was because I can write to you." He stared at her with that new adult look in his eyes. "I ain't no farmer, Easter. I goin' in the man's show," he told her.

She hugged him. "You know how to get back home, don't you, Jason?"

"Yes. And you always be in my mind."

Dr. Taylor smiled and nodded. She turned to him. "He can go. And, mister, you take good care of my Jason, hear?"

March 31, 1866
Dear Miss Grantley,

I hope this letter finds you enjoying the best of health. Please forgive me for taking so long to write to you, but it took me this long to make another decision. First, let me tell you how our town is coming along. We call it New Canaan. We have a church, a school, and we are building a molasses mill and a general store. Some of the people still work for the Williams family to make extra money for the land they purchased.

Miss Fortune moved to the cabin that was built next to the school especially for the teacher. We call it the teacher's house. The men and women take turns keeping guard, though, to make certain that the buckra don't come and burn down our school as they try to do last week. Miss Fortune smelled the smoke and saw the men who set the fire riding away. She say it look like they was wearing some kind of hood. Thank God we put the fire out before it made much damage. And to think we told her to come and live among us because we thought she would be safer with us than in the cottage near the big house!

Some bad news. Miriam and several other children died from a terrible fever. Brother Thomas still cannot talk and cannot walk by himself. But we pray that one day he'll be better.

Now for me and my life. I have decided, first, not to marry Julius but to go back to the old Rebel camp and find Mariah and Gabriel. Remember I tell you about them? If Obi is searching for me, he'll go to them because that's where he last left me. I went to the Freedmen's Bureau even though I said I wasn't going again, and I was told that they have a list from a colored regiment. They will write to me when they get more information.

Jason joined a medicine show. I got a letter from him and he says he is happy and fine. I miss him so much.

Now for the big news and decision: I want to go to the school in Philadelphia. We don't have enough schools or teachers to go around. Our small schoolhouse is full to overflowing, with some of the children coming from the Riverview plantation. Rose and Miss Fortune helped me to make up my mind to go to Philadelphia. Also, Miss Fortune said that I could live with her family while I attended the school. That made me feel less afraid about going. I have a welcome letter from her family already saying that I do not have to worry about my room or board.

So, my dear Miss Grantley, I hope you are as happy

and excited about my decision as I am. I hope it's not too late for me to attend the school. I saved a little bit of money, and Rose and a few of the other people want to help pay some of the costs too. I look forward to hearing from you soon. I am, as always,

> Your Friend and Student,
> Easter

Epilogue

March 1866

The tall young man gazed at the still waters gleaming in the sun. He'd found a quiet spot on the deck of the ship, away from the other soldiers. He removed his army jacket and pulled his cap over his deep-set eyes to shade them from the sun's glare.

He was glad to be coming home to South Carolina. A lone sea gull flew overhead, a sign that they would soon be nearing land. He closed his eyes and saw her little brown, heart-shaped face and her lively eyes. He wondered how much she'd changed these past few years and how long it would take to find her.

First he'd go to the Freedmen's Bureau in Charleston, and then to the old Confederate camp, where he had left her with Mariah and Gabriel. She may even have gone back to the Jennings farm, their former home. He would find her, though. No matter how long it took, he would find her.